The Cowboy's Gift-Wrapped Bride

VICTORIA PADE

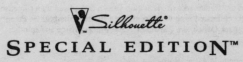

Silhouette®

SPECIAL EDITION™

Published by Silhouette Books

America's Publisher of Contemporary Romance

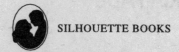

SILHOUETTE BOOKS

ISBN 0-373-24365-0

THE COWBOY'S GIFT-WRAPPED BRIDE

Visit Silhouette at www.eHarlequin.com

Printed in U.S.A.

Chapter One

Matt McDermot didn't need the voice coming from his truck radio to tell him he was in one of the worst blizzards Wyoming had ever suffered. He could see it for himself, right out his windshield. It was about all he could see as snow blew straight at him and left his visibility at maybe ten feet.

He was new to Wyoming. New to weather like this. He'd driven through Texas ice storms during his years growing up and living there with his family but even that hadn't been as bad.

Welcome to Wyoming, he thought, wondering if it had been such a good idea to move to the small town of Elk Creek after all.

Nah, on second thought he didn't really believe the move had been a bad idea. Not when all three of his brothers and his sister, too, were there. Not when it gave him a chance to get to know the grandfather he'd only met a few years ago.

And not when it gave him a chance to get far, far away from Sarah and the havoc she'd wreaked on his life.

Besides, he liked Elk Creek and up to now the change of seasons had been pretty pleasant. What was one bout of bad weather? Next time he'd just take the predictions more seriously than he had today.

But for now, here he was, only a few miles from Elk Creek and home, and he'd driven right into the worst of the storm.

If he hadn't stopped to put the chains on his tires he wouldn't be moving at all. And he had to keep moving, he knew, or risk not getting through.

The weatherman came on the radio again, announcing that this storm could dump a full thirty-six inches of the white stuff before the next day and another foot to two feet by the morning after that.

No doubt about it, they'd be having a white Christmas this year, the radio announcer promised, because even when the snow stopped, frigid temperatures were headed to the area for the week until the holiday. Which meant Cheyenne and its outlying suburbs and farmland would be in the deep freeze and wouldn't see much melting to speak of.

Matt didn't mind that part of things. He was looking forward to his first white Christmas. He just hoped he got back to the ranch in one piece to enjoy it.

The news report turned into a traffic update then, listing road closures due to high winds and drifting snow.

The highway Matt was driving wasn't on the list but probably only because it was an isolated country road without enough usage to get it mentioned on the radio.

"Or maybe it's officially closed and I just don't know it," he said to himself, realizing that his truck was the only vehicle on it.

But no sooner had he thought that than he spotted the weak flashing of red lights up ahead. They looked as if they might belong to another car but they seemed to be at an odd angle so he didn't veer toward them. Instead he concentrated on staying centered between the tall poles of the streetlights on either side of the highway—his only way of judging where the road was.

It was a good thing he didn't let the flashing lights throw him off course because as he neared them he saw that they were indeed coming from another vehicle—a small beige sedan that had gone into a ditch off the side of the road, nose-first in a deep drift.

Apparently the car had been there awhile because the battery was dying, the rear lights dimming even as Matt approached.

It was dangerous for him to stop and he knew it. A slow, steady progression was his best hope of getting through this storm. If his truck stalled in the cold or just got stuck in the snow that could drift around it within minutes, he would be stranded.

But what if the other car's driver or passengers were still in it?

It was possible they'd already been picked up by another passerby and had left the lights flashing to warn any oncoming vehicle, but the odds of that didn't seem good.

And Matt knew he couldn't drive by without checking for people who might be still inside and hurt from that deep dive into the ditch that left the car's rear end at a sharp upward pitch.

So he carefully came to a stop, turning on his own hazard lights and hoping they were bright enough to warn anyone else who might come up from behind him—as unlikely as it was that anyone else was crazy enough to be out in this mess.

He left his engine idling and reached across to the glove box, popping it open and retrieving a flashlight from inside.

It was only midafternoon but the clouds were so dense and the snow so thick—not to mention that it was piled up almost completely over the other car—that he thought he might need some extra light to see inside the vehicle.

He set the flashlight in his lap, flipped up the fleece collar of his suede shearling coat and pulled down on the brim of his Stetson to keep it securely on his head. Then he opened the door and hopped out of the truck into wind so fierce it had turned the snowflakes into shards of glass against his face.

Luckily he knew exactly where his shovel was—just behind the truck's cab—so he reached blindly for it with one gloved hand, pulling the tool out from beneath its wintry blanket.

Carrying the shovel and flashlight, Matt plowed through snow that was nearly knee-deep in some places, making his way as fast as he could to the side of the road.

The wind was a howl that obliterated any other sounds, but he was reasonably sure no one was calling for help from within the car. He had to dig to get to the driver's side door, then he managed to break its frozen seal and pull it open to shine the flashlight into the interior.

It was a good thing he'd taken the trouble.

Inside the car was a woman hunched over the steering wheel, her head bloody against the windshield.

She didn't move and Matt had a moment's sick feeling that he was too late.

He yanked off one glove and pressed two fingers to her neck, just under her jawbone.

There was still some warmth and softness to her skin, telling him right off the bat that she was alive, and when he found her pulse, he had it confirmed.

But she was hurt. There was no doubt about that. Badly enough to be unconscious.

He knew it wasn't good to move her but what choice did he have? Even if this had been a sunny day in May he'd have had to call for a helicopter rescue because they were too far from the nearest hospital for an ambulance to reach them with any speed. In this weather neither a helicopter nor an ambulance could risk it, so he was the only help this woman was going to get.

And the longer he spent pondering it, the more danger they were both in.

So he switched off the flashlight and slid it into his coat pocket, jammed the shovel into the snow like a stake claiming land and replaced his glove. Then he eased the woman out of the car and into his arms as cautiously as he could, gently hoisting her up against his chest like a fragile sack of grain.

She wasn't much bigger than a minute. He'd carried calves and foals that weighed more. But since she was still unconscious, she was dead weight.

Her head fell limply to his shoulder and her right arm swung outward like a loose gate. He kept his head hunched over her to provide as much protection as he could from the elements he knew were biting through the simple wool coat she had on. She wore no gloves to cover her hands or hat to conceal the long fall of curly burnished red hair.

She moaned when he lifted her into the passenger side of his truck, but she still didn't regain consciousness.

"You'll be okay. I'll get you to a doctor," he told her anyway, thinking maybe the reassurance would penetrate somehow. Then he reached behind the seat for the emergency blanket he kept there and covered her with it, cranking up the heat before he closed the door and went back to her car.

A quick scan of the inside of the topsy-turvy sedan showed him a black leather purse and a single suitcase on the rear floor.

There was no telling when anyone would be able to get out here again and he knew she was likely to need her things so he grabbed the purse and the suitcase to take along, too. Then he retrieved his shovel, closed the door and finally high-stepped his way to his truck once more, hoping he could make good time getting his unplanned passenger to help.

The first thing she was aware of was an unrelenting headache that started in her temple and wrapped around the side of her head like a vise.

The second thing she realized was that she was very, very cold even though it felt as if there were heavy blankets covering her. So cold her fingers and toes ached almost as bad as her head did.

She could hear the sound of voices and a telephone ringing, but it was all from a distance. Muted. She couldn't make out any of what the voices were saying.

She opened her eyes into slits that let in stabbing white light. But she couldn't bear the bright fluorescent glare and had to scrunch them closed again in a hurry.

That was when a deep male voice said, "Are you finally going to join us?"

The voice wasn't familiar. Not at all. But it was smooth and full-bodied and confident, and it reminded her of dark molasses.

Then she heard a few footsteps, a door opening and the same voice said, "I think she's coming to," before the click of boot heels brought the man to stand near her again.

Painful or not, she decided she didn't have any choice but to open her eyes again. By very, very slow increments, allowing in only as much of the light as she could endure and adjusting to it before raising her lids more, until she finally had them completely open.

She found herself looking up into a face of chiseled planes and rawboned, ruggedly masculine beauty.

"Don't be afraid, Jenn," the man said. "You're okay. You were in a car accident but you're safe now."

Jenn? Had he called her Jenn? The name didn't ring a bell.

"Jenn?" she repeated.

"We had to get into your purse and look at your driver's license to find out who you are. I'm sorry for poking into your things, but—"

"Jenn," she said again, alarm building in her voice to match what was building inside her as it began to sink in that the name didn't mean anything to her.

"Jenn Johnson—it's on your driver's license. Along with your picture."

"You think that's me? Jenn Johnson?"

"That's what we've pieced together. Isn't it right?"

"Is it?" she said with growing agitation. "I don't know."

"You don't know?"

Her heart was racing now. She could hear the rush of blood through her veins and it crossed her mind that maybe she was dreaming. Maybe she was having a very vivid nightmare. A very vivid nightmare in which she'd somehow forgotten who she was.

But her head hurt too much for this to just be a dream.

"I don't know if that's the right name or not. I don't know that name at all. I don't know if it's mine," she said, sounding on the verge of hysteria.

"You don't know who you are?" he asked as if he doubted his own comprehension of what she was saying.

"I really don't know!" she said, the full force of her own panic echoing in her voice.

He must have heard it, because he said, "Okay, okay. Don't get riled up. Your driver's license says you're Jenn Johnson," he said soothingly. "Your car went off the road in a snowstorm. I found you inside, slumped over the steering wheel, unconscious and bleeding from the head. I brought you here—you're in a doctor's office. No one recognized you from around these parts so we looked in your purse for identification and that's what we came up with—a Colorado driver's license with your picture on it that says you're Jenn Johnson." He explained everything in such detail, no doubt hoping it would make her recall something.

But it didn't. And she felt a fear so intense it was palpable.

She tried to sit up then to combat her own sense of extreme vulnerability.

But when she did, her head started to spin and she thought she'd pass out.

The man seemed in tune with what was going on with her because he stepped even closer to the examining table and put a steadying hand on her shoulder. "I think you'd better stay lying back until my brother gets a look at you. He's the doctor. We're in his office."

Something popped into her head then, as she looked at the man claiming to be her rescuer. But it didn't have anything to do with her. It was some kind of odd flash that instead made her think she knew *him*. Although that didn't make sense.

"Are you Matt McDermot?" she asked tentatively.

He looked almost as confused as she felt. "That's me," he confirmed.

"And we are in a place called Elk Creek? In Wyoming?"

"We are," he said.

"Did you just move here? From Texas?"

His lips stretched into a smile as his full eyebrows creased over dark green eyes the color of fir trees. "Right," he said, clearly surprised and somewhat confused.

Another of those strange flashes hit her, causing her to recall him saying his brother was the doctor here.

"Bax McDermot—is that your brother?"

"Did I hear someone say my name?"

The voice coming from another man suddenly standing in the doorway startled her so much she jolted as if she'd been hit. But one look at him and Jenn knew he was Matt's older brother.

He stepped into the room then with a warm, friendly smile on a face that bore a striking resemblance to Matt's.

And behind Bax McDermot came an attractive auburn-haired woman with topaz-colored eyes.

"Carly Winters," Jenn said as much to herself as to everyone else.

"You're close. Carly McDermot," the other woman amended.

"Of course," Jenn nearly whispered. "You just married the doctor."

The two new arrivals to the room both smiled but they looked as if they were waiting for the punch line to a joke.

The trouble was, the joke was on Jenn and it wasn't a very nice one. Her mouth went dry and her heart started to pound all over again in a fresh wave of alarm at the thought that she still couldn't tell them anything about herself.

"Uh, we have a bit of a hat trick going on here," Matt McDermot offered then, his expression once more showing his own confusion. "Our girl seems to know everyone but herself."

The intensely attractive cowboy went on to explain what had transpired since Jenn had regained consciousness. All the while Jenn let herself focus on him as if he were her anchor.

He was a big man with wide, straight shoulders and a broad chest that narrowed to a sharply V'd waist. His hips didn't have an ounce of spare flesh— or any room for more—in the tight jeans he wore along with the plaid flannel shirt that stretched across the muscles of his upper body.

And as for his face...well, it was about the best face she'd ever seen on a man. At least as far as she knew. With a high forehead and a long, thin, slightly pointed nose; straight, not-too-thin, not-too-full lips; a strong, square jawline; and a chin with a slight dent in the center of it.

He had great hair, too—thick, coarse and shiny golden-brown in color. He wore it short around the sides and a little spiky on top.

And there were also the eyes she'd noticed before. Slightly soulful, kind and amused at once, and as dark a green as a dense mountain forest.

When Matt McDermot had finished updating his brother, the doctor switched into a more businesslike mode, drawing Jenn's attention with questions aimed directly at her.

"You can't tell us anything about yourself? Where you live? If you were on your way to Elk Creek or would have just passed through?"

Jenn again tried to reclaim the information from the storehouse of her brain as Bax McDermot shined a light in her eyes and took a closer look into them. But it was as if that part of her mind was locked behind a steel door to which she didn't have the key.

"I know I should know and somewhere I do, but I can't get hold of it," she confessed with a hearty portion of frustration in her tone.

Bax McDermot shined the light higher up, into the hair he parted with his fingers, looking at about the spot from which her headache seemed to originate.

"How about numbers? Can you remember your phone number or your address?"

Once more Jenn tried. And failed. And felt another surge of panic at the further evidence that she didn't know the most rudimentary things about herself.

"Do you know your mother's name? Or your father's? Or a friend's?"

Jenn shook her head slowly, feeling tears of pure fear well up in her eyes. But she couldn't lie there and cry like a baby, she told herself. No matter how terrified she was of what was happening to her. So she worked hard to blink the moisture away and tried to keep her voice from quivering. "No. Nothing. I don't remember anything."

"Except a whole lot of details about us and our lives," Matt reminded from the opposite side of the examining table where he still stood, almost with an air of protectiveness.

"Do you know how you know so much about us?" Carly inquired.

But Jenn didn't have an answer for that, either. In fact, it was just another thing that unnerved her.

"Could you have been coming to Elk Creek to visit someone for Christmas?" Carly suggested in what seemed to be her capacity as assistant to her husband who was ordering Jenn to follow his finger with her eyes and generally examining her while they all talked.

"Christmas, "Jenn repeated. "Christmas is in a

week," she said, remembering that at least and hanging on to that small victory. "I guess I could have been coming to visit someone for the holiday." But that was as far as she could go in answering the other woman's question. And even that had no basis in fact.

"Do you think you've been to Elk Creek before?" Matt asked. "Maybe you grew up here or have family here?"

It was as if this had become a guessing game.

Jenn tried to play along, considering the possibilities presented to her as if she were trying on clothes to see how they fit. Wishing something *would* fit. But again she just drew a blank.

"I can't be sure if I've ever been here before or not. And as for family, I just don't know."

"How about anything about where you came *from?*" the doctor tried. "There's a Denver address on your driver's license but we haven't been able to try contacting anyone there because the phone lines are down. Do thoughts of Denver spark any memories?"

Jenn could only shake her head woefully.

"What do you think?" Matt's query was aimed at his brother, but Jenn's glance went to the doctor, too, hoping he had an answer not only to Matt's question, but to her own dilemma as well.

"I don't have a lot of experience with this but I'd say we're looking at selective amnesia," Bax McDermot said to the room in general. Then more directly to Jenn he said, "There weren't any signs of a concussion when I examined you when Matt brought you in and there still aren't now even though you took a bad bump on the head. And because it doesn't appear to be an injury serious enough to have caused the amnesia on its own, I'm wondering if you may have suffered something emotionally disturbing or traumatic. Maybe something that spurred you to come to Elk Creek in the first place if this is where you were actually headed. Maybe that, coupled with the blow to the head, has put you into a psychological amnesia. But one way or the other, amnesia is a tricky phenomenon that can obliterate certain parts of memory while other portions are left intact. I'm guessing that's what we're dealing with.''

"So what do we do about it?" Jenn asked, hating that she sounded so weak, so small, so afraid.

"We've already sent word to the sheriff. He'll be here any minute," Carly offered. "But what if we get a message to the local radio station and have them put out an announcement asking if anyone knows a Jenn Johnson?''

Both men agreed that was a good idea and Jenn was more than willing to go along with it. To embrace it, in fact, hoping someone would come forward and fill in a few blanks for her.

And while she waited, left alone in the examining room to rest, she put some effort into working up to sitting in a chair without feeling as if she might faint and regaining some warmth by sipping hot tea that Carly brought in to her.

When the sheriff arrived he asked her much the same questions the doctor had, with no more success. Then he confirmed that with the phone lines down their hands were tied for the time being in regards to trying to reach anyone in Denver. But he assured her that as soon as possible he'd do what he could.

Carly dug up a portable radio for Jenn to listen to after the sheriff left so she could hear the message the disc jockey sent out after each song. Over and over again the D.J. gave her name and pertinent information and asked anyone in town who knew anything about her to get word to the station.

But at the end of two hours there hadn't been any notification of either to the radio station or the doctor's office and it seemed clear that no one listening to the radio knew who Jenn Johnson was or why she'd come to Elk Creek.

And even though by then Jenn had managed to gain some control over her fear and come to grips with what was happening to her, she still felt like a lost puppy at the pound that nobody had claimed.

Until Matt McDermot seemed to do just that, reappearing from somewhere outside the examining room as sounds of the office closing for the day drifted in to her.

And even though she didn't understand it any more than she understood what was going on in her brain, seeing him again made her feel infinitely safer.

He leaned a broad shoulder against the door frame, crossed his arms over his chest and said, ''Doesn't look like anything's going to break for the time being to let us know who you are. Bax says what you really need for tonight is some sleep, so what would you say to coming out to the ranch and staying there until we sort through this or you get your memory back? There's plenty of room and nothin' we McDermots like better than having a pretty woman around or a puzzle to solve.''

"I seem to qualify as a puzzle all right."

He smiled, and when he did, the left side of his mouth went higher than the right, giving it an appealing tilt. "Is that a yes?"

She didn't have to think about it. Although maybe she should have when she realized that the thought of remaining anywhere near Matt McDermot went a long way toward making her feel better.

She didn't think about it, though. She just said, "That would be really nice. Thank you. And thank you for everything else, too. I think you saved me from freezing to death."

"It all worked out," he said, seeming slightly uncomfortable with her gratitude and with taking the credit he was due.

For a moment their eyes locked and Jenn felt a kind of connection to him that she couldn't fathom. A nice kind of connection that helped stave off the fear that kept threatening a return.

But Matt McDermot only lingered over that glance for a moment before he drew himself up to what looked to be his full six feet two or three inches of height and said, "Let's get going, then. Elk Creek's plow has just made a swipe at the roads so we should be able to reach the ranch if we leave before too much more snow accumulates."

And with that Jenn seemed to become Matt McDermot's charge.

Something that felt more right and more comforting than anything had since she'd opened her eyes.

She just hoped that she could trust her instincts more than she could trust her memory.

Chapter Two

Too much snow had already fallen for the plow to get down to bare pavement on the roads. Instead it had left them densely snowpacked with new drifts piling up to replace the old.

But inside Matt McDermot's truck the heater was on and the view through the windows was of pristine white flakes swirling in a mesmerizing dance.

And even though Jenn tried to stay awake, she just couldn't.

So one minute she was staring out at the golden swath the headlights cut through the snow and the next thing she knew Matt McDermot's deep molasses voice was saying, "Jenn? Wake up. We're here."

She apparently hadn't been asleep long enough to

have forgotten who he was or the fact that they were going to the McDermot ranch where she'd been offered refuge because when she awoke it wasn't to any kind of startled confusion about where she was or whom she was with. Instead she slipped out of sleep to the irresistible lure of that rich voice that seemed to roll over her in a sweet, beckoning refrain. And Jenn's first thought was that she should probably feel less comfortable and at ease with this man who she had just met.

She didn't, though.

When she did open her eyes this time it was to the view from the passenger side window. And what she saw was a big ranch-style house with a covered porch that wrapped around twin wings stretching out on either side of the main entrance. All the porch railings and pillars were wound with evergreen boughs and tiny white lights, and more tiny white lights dripped from all the eaves, turning the snow that blanketed the place into glimmering crystal.

It was a warm, welcoming sight.

"When Buzz Martindale owned this ranch the house was only a small two-bedroom farmhouse," Jenn said, the words spilling out as if from a speech she somehow knew by rote. "But after he turned the place over to his grandchildren—and you all became wildly successful with a new breed of hardy cattle—the original house was turned into not much more than the entryway to the addition that made the place one of the nicest homes in Elk Creek."

"Maybe in your real life you do a nightclub act as a psychic," Matt said with a slight, stunned laugh. "Are you having visions of this stuff or what?"

Jenn shrugged. "I don't know. The information is just there. Nothing else is, but these thoughts keep popping into my head from out of nowhere."

"Does the place seem familiar? Maybe you were here before for some reason?"

"Sorry," she said as if another negative answer would disappoint him.

"Well, you're right about it, anyway," he confirmed, being a good sport.

"Buzz moved away with his wife for a while— if I'm not mistaken—and that was when he gave the ranch up to his grandchildren."

Matt nodded. "My grandmother was sick and they moved to Denver to be nearer the hospital where she was being treated."

"And after she died he stayed on in Denver," Jenn continued, "until he broke his leg and couldn't care for himself anymore."

"He broke his knee. His right knee."

"And he's been back here ever since. Doing well."

"Amazing," Matt said, more to himself than to her.

"And weird," Jenn added, wondering at herself as much as he obviously was.

She'd been looking at the house the whole time but now she turned her head to find Matt studying her through the darkness that was only broken by the Christmas lights on the house.

His expression made it evident he was curious but

he didn't appear to be suspicious. Although she wouldn't have blamed him if he had been. It suddenly occurred to her that if she kept it up she might cause him to be.

"Maybe I shouldn't say these things out loud," she said, thinking the minute the words were spoken that maybe she shouldn't have said that, either.

"I figure you shouldn't stifle whatever comes into your mind. You never know when one thing might spark memory of another or give us an idea of what's going on with you and why you're here."

She was grateful for that. Not because it seemed important that she be able to go on with these bouts of trivia but because he didn't think she was some kind of lunatic or con artist pulling a scam—what he could well have thought if he were another sort of person.

But as it was, those dark green eyes of his merely scanned her face as if she were a riddle he was trying to figure out and a clue might be there for him to read.

And as the intensity of that gaze washed over her, Jenn felt a tingling response sluice along her nerve endings. A response she didn't understand any more than she understood what was going on with her memory.

But the one thing she *did* know was that this was no time to be basking in a man's glance. Or voice. Or company.

"Shouldn't we go in?" she asked then in an attempt to escape the close confines of the truck cab and the enticing scent of a citrusy, clean-smelling aftershave that was only making it more difficult for her to think straight.

''Sure,'' Matt agreed.

He turned off the truck's engine and got out without a moment's hesitation, coming to the passenger side from around the rear to open her door.

When he had, he offered her a hand to help her down, and before she'd considered whether or not it was wise to take it, Jenn did.

But that physical contact didn't help her already jumbled thoughts because the moment her hand connected with his much larger, callused one, more of that odd tingling sensation began, shooting all the way up her arm this time.

The reaction didn't make any more sense to her now than it had when she'd experienced it as a result of nothing more than his gaze. The only conclusion she could come to to explain it was that something purely elemental, something perfectly primitive, was afoot.

But why now and not when he'd placed a steadying hand to her shoulder at his brother's office when she'd tried to sit up and felt faint?

In the office there hadn't been bare skin against bare skin the way there was now....

Jenn was tempted to indulge in the feeling, to let her hand stay nestled within his, to go on letting the heat of that naked flesh seep into every pore.

But the temptation—along with the pleasure that was skittering all through her—was also very alarming. After all, this man was a stranger to her and certainly the circumstances they were currently in—or at least the circumstances she was currently in—were not conducive to any kind of attraction between them.

So the moment her feet were firmly planted on the ground she pulled her hand out of his as if she'd just been singed by hot coals. For surely it seemed as if she was just as likely to get burned.

If Matt noticed anything amiss in her withdrawal, he didn't show it. He just stepped around her and grabbed her suitcase and purse from the truck's bench seat.

Then he closed the door, turned to face the house and said, "Ladies first," in a friendly way that held no hint that he'd had the same response to her that she'd had to him.

But then, why would something as innocuous as their hands touching affect him the way it had affected her? It was only things in *her* head that were haywire.

Accepting that as a fact she couldn't do anything about at the moment, Jenn opted for ignoring it and took the lead to the house, being careful not to slip on the walkway that had been shoveled at some point but was once again covered in snow.

When they reached the double front doors with their elaborate ovals of stained glass in the top halves, Matt went ahead of her to open one for her.

"There you go," he said to urge her inside.

Jenn stepped into a big brightly lit foyer and felt a blast of heat that chased the chill back outside before Matt closed the door.

"We've missed supper by now," he said then.

"So how about I show you to your room and give you half an hour to settle in? Then we can meet in the kitchen and I'll rustle us up something to eat."

There were voices coming from somewhere toward the rear of the house and what sounded like post-meal cleanup. No one was in sight but Jenn was having another of those informational blips about who those voices likely belonged to.

Not that they seemed familiar, but for some reason she had a pretty good idea of who lived in this house.

She opted for keeping it to herself though and merely said, "That sounds good."

Matt pointed his dimpled chin to the left where Jenn was reasonably certain a hallway that matched the one on the right would take her to the left wing she'd seen from outside. "I'll put you up in the room next to mine. It's straight down there, the third door."

Again he waited for her to precede him.

Old-fashioned cowboy courtesy, Jenn thought.

It was nice. And as she once more took the lead down the hall, she wondered if he was this way with all women and if he was, why someone hadn't snapped him up for herself by now so they could be treated like royalty all the time.

"Each one of these is a private suite," Matt said as he opened the third door for her. "We—that is, my grandfather and all my siblings—use the kitchen, dining room, living room and rec room— they're communal. But we each have a suite with a bedroom and a private bath, along with a sitting room so we can hole up in our own space if we've a mind to. There are even doors from the suites out to the porch if anybody wants to come and go that way, too.''

Jenn entered the sitting room portion of her newly appointed rooms. A pale blue overstuffed couch and chair and an oval coffee table monopolized the space, positioned to face a stone fireplace on the outside wall where French doors did indeed lead to that wraparound porch.

It was a cozy room, especially with the window on the other side of the fireplace framing a view of a huge oak tree whose branches were all snow-kissed.

''The bedroom's in here,'' Matt said, taking her suitcase through another door that connected a large room furnished with a queen-sized bed covered in a downy blue checked quilt. There was also a desk and dressing table, a large bureau with a mirror above it, and another full-length mirror on the opposite door that apparently led to that bathroom he'd mentioned.

''Make yourself at home,'' Matt said after he'd set her suitcase and purse on the bed. ''Will you be okay on your own for a while?''

''I'll be fine.'' She marveled at the stroke of luck it had been that someone like Matt McDermot had found her on the side of the road. She really wasn't clearheaded enough to have fended for herself and another person might have taken advantage rather than looked after her so conscientiously and generously.

But before she could tell him how much she appreciated all he was doing for her, he said, "You can get to the kitchen by going the rest of the way down that hallway we just used. You'll pass the rec room and then you can't miss the kitchen. I'll be there when you're ready."

He left and Jenn felt a little like Alice after she'd gone through the looking glass.

Trying to get past how dazed she still felt, she took off her coat and stared down at her clothes, realizing for the first time that there were blood spatters on her white blouse and gray slacks—blood spatters that matched those on her coat—from where her head had been cut open in the accident.

She certainly didn't want to stay in stained clothing so she slipped off her black loafers and intended to shed the rest of her soiled garments when she suddenly wondered what she looked like. Because now that she thought about it, she didn't have a clear image in her mind of even *that*.

So she crossed to the full-length mirror on the bathroom door for a look.

She wasn't tall—that was the first thing that registered. Probably about five-four if she stood straight. She was just about average weight. Except that her feet were somewhat on the large side and her breasts weren't.

Her skin was clear and not so pale that it had a bluish tinge the way the skin of some redheads did. But still she was pretty fair. Her complexion was clear though, which pleased her. And her features were devoid of any enormous flaws. Well, maybe the cheekbones were on the high side, but that was good.

Her eyes were a nice shade of dark blue. With lashes that were long enough to be notable.

Probably the thing she liked best in her assessment of herself was her hair. It fell a few inches past her shoulders in a thick, wavy mass of burnished red that had a richness to it rather than an orange tint.

Of course at that moment it was kind of a mess, between the accident, the blood from the cut that had matted it just inside her hairline and then the haphazard washing it had taken at the doctor's office.

She would have liked to shampoo her whole head before she went out to see Matt again but that couldn't be done in half an hour so she decided it would just have to be brushed well and pulled back.

With that—and getting a change of clothes—in mind, she went to open her suitcase where Matt had left it on the bed.

While she was rummaging around in it for a hairbrush, she kept an eye out for any clue as to who she was, what kind of life she'd left behind, or why she'd come to this small town.

But she didn't see anything remarkable or unusual inside the suitcase. It held only ordinary clothes, mostly jeans, sweaters and turtleneck shirts, with the exception of a simple jumper and a pair of velvet overalls.

There was also a pair of casual black suede slip-on shoes and a pair of low-heeled pumps. A few lacy bras and matching panties. Some socks, and that was about all.

But after suffering a little disappointment that there hadn't been anything very telling in the suitcase she realized that there were some things the items didn't say that were an indication of what *wasn't* going on with her. For instance the only nightgown and robe she had were plaid flannel and there wasn't a single slinky, sexy dress in the lot. So clearly she hadn't come to Elk Creek for a romantic rendezvous.

She finally found a clear plastic makeup bag in one of the suitcase's side pockets and even before she took it out she could see a comb and brush in it, along with some makeup and toiletries. But when she pulled the bag free of its cloth cubby she found something else behind it. Something that seemed odd.

A beat-up shaving kit.

The brown leather was soiled and ashy, and one side showed signs of having been crushed and then pulled back into a semblance of its original shape.

Jenn pulled it out, reassessing the other articles of the suitcase to be certain that nothing else in it belonged to a man.

It didn't.

So why did she have this ratty old Dopp kit?

She set it on top of the other things in the suitcase so she could open it. It wasn't easy. The zipper was rusty and stubborn. But she finally managed to force its teeth apart.

And when she did, what she found inside was not shaving gear.

The kit was full of money.

Lots of it.

Jenn turned the shaving kit upside down and shook it, causing a fluttering green rain of bills to fall onto the quilt.

There wasn't anything else in the kit. Just cash.

She did a quick count—$2,157—none of it in anything larger than a twenty.

Traveling money? Her savings? Or maybe moving money? Maybe she'd been on her way to Elk Creek to live.

But would she have traveled with so much cash? And if she'd been moving to Elk Creek, why did she only have one small suitcase rather than a whole carload of belongings?

Maybe she'd come to Elk Creek to buy something. But why in cash? If she were making a large purchase wouldn't she use a check or a credit card?

Maybe. Maybe not. Maybe the seller wanted cash.

But the one thing that made none of those possibilities click in her mind was that something about the money triggered an unpleasant feeling in Jenn. She couldn't put her finger on why, but she had the sense that it wasn't hers.

And that gave her pause.

Because if the money wasn't hers, then whom did it belong to? And why did she have it?

Of course just a sense that it wasn't her money and a bad feeling about it didn't make it true. Maybe it *was* hers but it was all she had in the world because she'd lost her job and needed to start a whole new life. Maybe what she'd been feeling before the accident was depression or despondency or natural concern and so the money had triggered a negative feeling now as a remnant of all that.

But somehow she didn't believe it.

She didn't feel any kind of ownership over the cash. Instead she felt as if she wanted to hide it away. As if she were ashamed of it.

And why would she be ashamed of it unless it was ill-gotten gains of some kind?

That thought didn't sit well, either.

Was she a thief?

Oh dear.

What if she was a horrible person who had stolen money? Or swindled someone out of it? What if she hadn't been headed to Elk Creek at all but had just been on her way through it to somewhere else? Somewhere she was running to escape something terrible she'd done?

Except if that was the case, why did she know so much about Elk Creek and the people who lived there?

But then *that* had been the million-dollar question all along.

Or maybe it was just the $2,157 question.

So what was she going to do with it? she asked herself as she stood there staring down at all that cash on the bed.

She didn't know much, but suddenly she was very sure of one thing: It didn't seem like a good idea to tell Matt McDermot or anyone else about it.

It was possible that she couldn't really trust everyone around her, that someone might help themselves to the money if they knew it existed.

Okay, maybe now she *was* being crazy. She didn't actually believe anyone—especially Matt McDermot—would take anything from her.

On the other hand, she couldn't help being concerned with what Matt might think about it—and her—if she also let him know her negative feelings about the money.

Sure, he might give her the benefit of the doubt. To a man with his kind of wealth $2,157 wasn't that big a deal. It probably *was* just traveling money to him.

But what if he *didn't* think that? What if he thought she might have come by it by less than honest means?

It was bad enough to worry that she might be a thief, but to have Matt even consider that a possibility, too? To have his opinion of her tinged?

She just couldn't stand that idea.

Not that it had anything to do with that warm, tingly feeling she'd had earlier in the truck on the way home or when she'd taken his hand to get out of it, she reassured herself. Those feelings had just been part of the mental fog she'd been in since regaining consciousness.

She just didn't want to inspire any mistrust on his part. After all, she was a guest in his house. A perfect stranger he was allowing into his home, around his family.

And she needed his hospitality. His help. Certainly she didn't want to alienate him.

So that was all there was to it. She was sure of it.

She gathered up the money in a hurry, as if someone might come in any moment and see it, and she stuffed it back into the shaving kit. Then she hid the shaving kit deep beneath the clothes in her suitcase.

Maybe the sense that the money didn't belong to her was a mistake anyway, she thought as she did. It wasn't as if she were cooking on all burners. She was recognizing people she didn't know even while she couldn't remember her own name. She was attracted to a man she'd just met. A man she'd just met under the worst of circumstances. So who was to say that nothing more than a bad feeling about the money gave any credence to its origin or what her having it meant?

"It's probably nothing awful," she said out loud, as if that would chase away her negative feelings.

It didn't, though.

Something about that money rubbed her the wrong way.

But it was better that it rubbed her the wrong way than that it rubbed Matt McDermot the wrong way.

Because as much as she wished it weren't so, the one thing she knew without a doubt was that she cared a whole lot about what he thought of her.

A whole lot more than she wanted to care....

Chapter Three

Matt didn't ordinarily shave at eight o'clock at night. Unless there was something special going on, he didn't usually shave more than once a day.

But there he was, standing in front of the mirror in his bathroom, shaving. At eight o'clock at night. With nothing special going on.

Well, not anything he would have normally considered special, like a holiday or a dinner or a meeting or a party or a date.

It had been one hell of a day, though, he had to admit. Driving through a blizzard. Pulling an unconscious woman out of a snow-buried car. Finding out that that woman didn't remember who she was but that she did know who *he* was, and who Bax and Carly and Buzz were. Bringing that woman home with him...

Definitely not a run-of-the-mill day.

But no real reason to shave at the end of it, either.

So why was he doing it? he asked himself.

"As if you don't know," he answered, speaking to his reflection as if it were another person in the room.

He was shaving because in just a few minutes he'd be sitting down to supper with Jenn Johnson.

Not that Matt was happy to admit that that was his motivation. Because he wasn't.

It was one thing to help someone who was hurt and stranded in a snowstorm, to bring her home with him when she had nowhere else to go. That had only been the neighborly thing to do and Matt was nothing if not neighborly.

But it was something else again to be shaving for her.

And thinking about her every minute since he'd set eyes on her.

Those were above and beyond the call of being neighborly. And he knew it.

Yet there he was, doing both.

And why? Was it going to help her remember who she was? Was it going to give him some idea of why she'd been on her way into or passing through Elk Creek?

No. His shaving didn't serve any purpose at all.

Except that he didn't want her to see him whiskered and wild-looking.

He didn't want any pretty woman to see him whiskered and wild-looking.

And Jenn was a pretty woman. Damn beautiful, in fact.

And that was the crux of things, wasn't it? She was a beautiful woman and even showing the wear and tear of a bad day she'd been pretty enough to leave him struggling to keep his eyes off her.

Trim and petite, with those perky little breasts just hinting from behind her shirt in a way that stirred up a man without even trying.

And all that red hair…. It was the color of the paprika that Junebug, the McDermot housekeeper, put on her deviled eggs.

And Jenn's skin—that was like porcelain. Pure, flawless, luminous porcelain.

And that small, perfectly shaped nose.

And those soft, pink lips that were meant for kissing.

And those eyes…

Oh, yeah, those eyes…

The blue of a clear sky at twilight out on the range where no city lights diluted the rich, deep, deep hue…

Those eyes had just pulled him right in the minute they'd opened and he'd had his first look at them.

Not that he'd wanted to notice anything he'd noticed. Because he hadn't. Any more than he wanted to be picturing it all again in his mind's eye now.

He wanted to just see her as a passing stranger in need of a little assistance. Tall, short; thin, fat; beautiful or homely as a mud fence—he didn't want it to make any difference to him one way or another.

"So don't let it make any difference," he ordered his refection as he scraped off the last of the shaving foam with his razor.

What he wanted—what he *needed*—was to put Jenn Johnson into perspective, he decided. And to remember a few things himself. Like the vow he'd made that the next woman he got involved with would be someone he knew like the back of his hand. Someone who had no secrets. Someone so open she verged on the boring.

Because getting burned by a secretive woman once was enough. There was no way he wanted anything to do with any woman he couldn't read like a book.

And even though Jenn Johnson wasn't purposely keeping secrets from him the way Sarah had, Jenn certainly wasn't a woman he could read like a book. She was a woman who couldn't even recall her own name.

So helping her out, giving her aid and comfort and a roof over her head—those things were just being neighborly and they were okay.

But thinking about her as much as he'd thought about her since he'd found her, feeling that old familiar eagerness in the pit of his stomach, shaving for her at eight o'clock at night and counting the minutes until he could meet up with her again in the kitchen—those were not so okay with him.

Matt washed his face a little rougher than was

called for, as if the force could wipe away all those other things he wanted stopped.

He'd be damned if he'd let his inclinations toward Jenn Johnson have reign over him the way his inclination toward Sarah had had reign over him. He'd be damned if he'd invest any kind of emotions in her or let himself get lost in that curly paprika-red hair or those incredible twilight-blue eyes or that porcelain skin he was itching to touch.

He'd been a sap for a beautiful woman once and once was enough. He was nobody's fool. He'd graduated magna cum laude from Texas A&M. He had a master's degree in agriculture and animal husbandry. He'd run two ranches. He'd helped his older brothers come up with a new, heartier breed of cattle. He was a man who knew himself, who knew what he wanted out of life and where he was headed, and neither of those things included another woman he didn't know backward and frontward, inside and out. And that was all there was to it.

He sloshed cold water on his face, committed to not losing one ounce of control to thoughts about Jenn Johnson in any personal sense. Because he was damn sure not going to think about her like that.

He was going to think about ways to figure out who she was and where she ought to be and who she ought to be with, and that was all.

That was definitely all.

But even as he swore to himself that he wasn't going to get involved with her, another thought played at the back of his mind, taunting him.

Chemistry was chemistry.

And there just might be no small amount of it riding roughshod over him.

Regardless of what he vowed to himself or how strong his controls and convictions.

When Jenn stepped out of the bedroom half an hour later she'd changed into a heavy wool turtleneck sweater and a pair of jeans. She'd washed her face and reapplied some mascara and blush, and pulled her hair back into an oversized clip that left a spray of curls at her crown.

Nothing fancy. But at least she'd cleaned up and was more presentable than she had been.

Following Matt's instructions, she went the rest of the way down the hall to the rear of the house until she found the brightly lit kitchen. The voices and sounds of clattering dishes that she'd heard when she'd arrived were gone now and so were the people making them. Instead only Matt McDermot was there, pulling containers from the refrigerator several feet across the room. He was so intent on what he was doing that he didn't notice her standing in the doorway.

He'd cleaned up, too. His hair was somewhat less spiky than before and his handsome face was freshly shaved.

And the moment Jenn set eyes on him she felt that odd tingling sensation run through her again.

Of course it didn't help matters that he repeatedly bent over to reach into the refrigerator and a terrific derriere took center stage.

She might have watched him much longer but

from the doorway on the opposite side of the kitchen an elderly man came in, spotting her immediately.

"There she is," he said as if he and Matt had been wondering what was taking her so long.

"Buzz Martindale." Jenn christened him.

"Yep, that's me all right," he confirmed as he limped into the kitchen on a cane, favoring his right leg. "And Matt says you're Jenn Johnson. Havin' some head problems, are you?"

"It seems so," she confirmed, going farther into the kitchen herself until they met at the counter where Matt was taking dishes down from a cupboard after tossing her a welcoming smile that seemed to draw her to him.

"How are you feelin'?" Matt asked, giving her the once-over with those forest-green eyes.

"The headache is better than it was. Still there, but better. The dizziness comes and goes. An ache seems to be settling into my neck and shoulders but I'm not so cold anymore." Although being near him seemed to be what chased away the chills. Not that she'd ever say that, or even acknowledge it to herself.

"The neck and shoulder ache is prob'ly stress," Buzz offered. "A good night's sleep'll get rid of that for you. Always helps me when I get it."

"I'm sure you're right. Your grandson the doctor checked out my neck and said he didn't see any indication of whiplash," Jenn told him.

Buzz was staring at her openly. Studying her. Maybe sizing her up.

It made Jenn uncomfortable.

"What can I do to help?" she asked Matt, thinking she'd rather be moving around than merely standing there being looked at like a specimen in a petri dish.

"Take what you can carry over to the table and sit down. I'll do the rest," Matt answered.

The table was a huge rectangle nestled within the arms of a breakfast nook at one end of the kitchen. It took up a full six feet of corner space in a U that would surely seat a dozen or more people comfortably.

Jenn set out the two plates, silverware and napkins she'd brought with her, placing one on the end and the other just around the corner. Then she slid in to sit behind it.

Buzz joined her, sitting at the other end of the U, but sideways so he could stretch his leg out along the bench seat as if that eased an ache of his own.

He was still studying her. Scrutinizing her, really.

"You look a little familiar," he finally decreed. "I'm bettin' you were headed for Elk Creek, not just passin' through. Prob'ly to see family."

Matt made three trips bringing fried chicken, coleslaw, biscuits, mashed potatoes and gravy, honey and two glasses of water to the table before he slipped into the breakfast nook, too.

"Who's she look like, then?" he asked as the old man continued to study Jenn.

"Don't know. But she looks familiar. Name doesn't ring a bell, though. No Johnsons 'round here. Maybe you lived in Elk Creek as a girl and Johnson's yer married name."

"Married?" Matt repeated as if he didn't like the idea.

But then, for some reason, neither did Jenn.

"I don't think I'm married," she said with more forcefulness than was warranted. "I mean, I don't *feel* married and there's no wedding ring or mark on my wedding finger left by a ring. And there's also no pictures in my wallet of a husband or kids."

"And a husband would have missed her by now," Matt added as he filled both his plate and hers with food. "Either she'd have been meeting him or he would have wanted her to call when she got where she was going to make sure she'd made it through this storm. And I just checked in with the sheriff a few minutes ago—nobody's contacted him lookin' for her. Granted, the phone lines are still down."

"Could be a husband she left and he ain't lookin' fer her."

"I don't feel married," Jenn repeated, thinking that if she were married, surely she wouldn't be so attracted to Matt McDermot.

"How's 'bout signs of childbirth? Got any of them stretch marks?"

"Buzz!" Matt chided his grandfather.

"Well, that'd be a clue, wouldn't it?" the old man defended.

Jenn knew her face was coloring but she answered Buzz's question anyway. "No, no stretch marks." And she would have seen them if any existed because when she'd changed her clothes she'd checked out her body thoroughly to familiarize herself with it, finding not only no stretch marks but a narrow waist and a taut, flat stomach.

"Prob'ly no kids, then," Buzz concluded from what she'd said about having no stretch marks. "How's 'bout any birthmarks or scars?"

"None of those, either."

"Got any tattoos?"

"Jeez, Buzz," Matt groaned, rolling his eyes.

But Jenn only laughed at that one. "No, no tattoos, either."

"How many toes you got? Knew a family moved on a long time ago—everyone of 'em had six toes on each foot."

Jenn laughed again, enjoying the elderly man despite his bluntness. "Sorry. Only five per foot."

"And you ain't got that rosy hook-nosed beak of the Masseys from way back, so you prob'ly don't belong to them neither."

Buzz continued in that vein all the while Jenn and Matt ate, quizzing her, staring at her, trying to figure out who she was.

But he never did.

"Nope, can't place you," he finally concluded when both Matt and Jenn had finished eating. "There's somethin' 'bout you tickles my brain, though. I just can't put my finger on it."

"Maybe it'll come to you," Matt suggested.

"Sooner or later," Buzz agreed. "I'll keep workin' on it." The elderly man craned around to look at the clock on the back wall of the breakfast nook and then pushed himself to the end of the seat and used his cane to help himself get to his feet. "But now it's time for my program. Think I'll watch it under my heat blanket in bed.''

"Good idea," Matt said, although he watched the old man with fondness and didn't seem eager for him to go. "'Night, Buzz."

"'Night. See you in the mornin'." Then to Jenn he said, "And don't worry 'bout nothin', girl. You're welcome to stay here long as you need to."

"Thank you," she said, telling the older man good-night as he limped out of the kitchen.

"Sorry about that stretch-mark business earlier," Matt said when his grandfather was out of earshot.

"That's okay. He was right. It would have been a sign of having kids. But there aren't any," she reiterated. "And even though I know it isn't really a basis for anything, I honestly don't have any sense of being married, either, so I really don't think I am."

Matt just nodded his head, accepting her conclusion but not necessarily committing to it. "Buzz will likely come up with something. He may not be young but he's still sharp as a tack."

"Do you always call him by his first name?" Jenn asked then, curious about it.

"I guess we all do."

"Is that a remnant of not having known him when you were growing up?"

Once again Matt looked baffled. "You know about that, too?"

"I know he didn't like the man your mother wanted to marry—your father—so she eloped and didn't have anything to do with Buzz or her mother for years and years. That when they finally healed the rift she had a whole family of grown sons and a daughter that Buzz had never met before. But that you've all become close now.''

"Sometimes this is a little eerie,'' was Matt's only comment, referring to the facts about his family.

But his remark again gave Jenn second thoughts about the wisdom of spewing this information she had without knowing where it came from and so she changed the subject.

"Where is everybody else?'' she asked. "From the sounds I heard when we came in tonight I expected a lot of people to be around. Did I scare them all away?''

"No. My brothers went out to shovel the walks, and their wives and my sister decided to stay out of the way for the night so they didn't overwhelm you right off the bat, when you've already had a tough day.''

Matt mimicked his grandfather by glancing up at the clock. "And speaking of which, I think we should get you to bed.''

Jenn had to admit—to herself if not to him—that she'd begun to feel as if she were wilting.

"Let's do the dishes and then I will,'' she said.

"No way. No dishes for you. But how 'bout I make you a cup of tea with honey and lemon to take to bed with you?''

"That sounds good.''

Matt grabbed the honey pot and as many dishes

as he could carry and slid out of the nook. "Sit tight while I get your tea ready," he ordered.

Jenn didn't protest. She was suddenly feeling very weak and worn-out and she honestly didn't know if she had the strength to do more than get back to her bedroom. So she did as she'd been told and sat tight as Matt put the dirty dishes in the sink and filled a mug with water to heat in the microwave.

Then he took a fresh lemon from the refrigerator, washed it thoroughly and rolled it against the wooden cutting board with his palm and the heel of his hand before slicing a wedge from it.

Jenn knew she was really tired because something about his actions almost hypnotized her and she ended up watching his every move in silence.

Mainly her focus was on his hands. Big, capable hands that seemed to dwarf everything they came into contact with.

And in Jenn's mind she pictured him rolling the strained muscles of her shoulders the way he'd rolled the lemon—pushing with his palm and the heel of his hand in a gentle, insistent, adept massage.

Those hands would be strong against her tight muscles. Firm. Tender. They'd squeeze the stress out of her the same way they squeezed the juice from the lemon, with just the right amount of pressure.

And she'd grow pliable beneath his touch. She'd melt inside and her head would fall back and she'd give herself over to those hands...

"Here you go. All set."

Jenn didn't know when she'd drifted off into

some kind of trance but the sound of Matt's voice brought her out of it and she snapped to attention, raising her gaze to a face too handsome to help matters.

"Are you all right? You look kind of flushed," he said.

Great. He'd noticed the blush that she could feel flooding her face for the second time that evening and Jenn wondered if he could see past it into her wayward mind and figure out what she'd been thinking to cause it.

"I'm okay. Tired and dizzy again is all," she lied to hide what was really going on with her. But then what else could she do? She couldn't admit that she'd been fantasizing about him, could she?

"Let's get you to your room," he said, sounding concerned and making Jenn feel guilty for misleading him.

But she did need to get back to her room and away from this man and his effect on her, there was no doubt about that. So she slid around the bend of the bench seat.

Unfortunately it was right into Matt's waiting hand at her arm to help her up.

Not a good thing. Because this time, even through her clothes, a single touch of one of those hands she'd just been daydreaming about set off a whole new and more powerful set of tingles all through her.

"I'm okay," she insisted as she got to her feet, hoping he would let go.

He didn't, though. He kept hold of her, guiding

and supporting her all the way back to her bedroom and to the side of the bed.

He set the mug of hot tea on the nightstand and said, "Can you get yourself undressed and into bed or do you need help?"

Oh, what flashed through her mind at *that* suggestion!

Matt undressing her. His hands on her bare skin. Scooping her up into his arms to lie her gently on the bed. Getting into bed with her...

"No! Thank you. I'll be fine."

She'd answered too frantically and he seemed to think she was afraid of him.

He took a step backward, as if distance might help calm her fears. "My sister Kate or one of my sisters-in-law could come and help if you needed it. I didn't mean that I—"

"I know you didn't," Jenn was quick to assure him. "It's just that I don't need any help. But really, I can't tell you how much I appreciate everything you've done for me today."

"It was nothin'," he said, still watching her and no doubt wondering if she really was all right or if the bump on her head had made her lose her mind.

But then that was something she was wondering herself.

He must have decided the best thing was to leave her to her own devices because he said, "If you have any problems during the night, just holler. I'm next door and I'll hear you."

"Thanks. But I'm sure I'll be okay."

He took another long, hard look at her then, as if

to convince himself she was telling the truth, and those deep, dark green eyes seemed to emit the same kind of heat she'd imagined feeling from his touch, the kind she'd felt when his hand had taken hers to help her from the truck and again when he'd walked her to her bedside.

And in that moment she felt all the more certain that she just couldn't be married and still feel the way this man made her feel.

"Well, all right, then," he finally said, as if giving in against his will to leaving her alone. "Feel better."

"I'm sure I will. I just need some sleep."

"'Night, then."

"Good night."

Matt turned to leave and Jenn watched him go. She devoured every step of those long legs until he was out of her room and the door was closed behind him.

And then Jenn deflated, falling more than sitting on the edge of the bed, feeling every bit as weak as she'd claimed.

Except she wasn't so sure that the weakness had come from her car accident or her bump on the head or the incredible things that had come out of them both.

Instead it seemed as if her weakness was more *for* Matt McDermot than *from* anything that had happened to her.

And that was every bit as unnerving as not being able to remember who she was.

Chapter Four

It was midmorning when Jenn woke up the next day. She'd slept nearly twelve hours and she felt rested and much stronger than she had the evening before.

But as she rolled onto her back in bed and opened her eyes to acclimate herself, she recalled a dream she'd had several times during the night. A dream of herself as an old woman. An old woman here in this house, but not in this house the way it was now. And not because she belonged in it.

Strange. It felt as if there was something very strange about that dream. Even stranger than the dream itself. But since not one whit of her memory had returned as she'd slept, she didn't know why the dream seemed strange or if it was telling her something.

Lying in bed thinking about it didn't give her any answers and she was already embarrassed to have slept as late as she had, so she decided she couldn't stay there pondering it.

Instead she sat up and gingerly swung her legs over the side of the mattress. She wasn't sure if her head would pound again or if her neck and shoulders would still ache or if she'd still feel as weak. But all the remnants of the accident were gone and she felt fine.

Well, as fine as a person could feel when she didn't remember who she was.

Fine enough for a shower and a good shampoo, although she had to be careful about that because she still had a pretty good gash from her temple into her hairline.

Once she was finished with her shower, she dressed in jeans and a rolled-neck gray sweater with an argyle pattern on the front. She applied a little blush and mascara to put some color into her still slightly wan face and then blew her hair dry and pulled it back with an elastic scrunchie only inches from the ends in back.

When she judged herself presentable, she opened the heavy drapes that covered the windows.

Outside the sky was just as gray and overcast as it had been the day before, although the pristine whiteness of the snow that blanketed everything helped to brighten things considerably.

The wind didn't seem to be blowing anymore but

flakes were still falling, adding to what she guessed to be about three feet of snow already piled up.

It made for a beautiful sight, though. Clean. Quiet. Peaceful. A good day to be inside, all cozy and comfortable and warm.

She saw two men in the distance then, heading for the state-of-the-art barn, but they were too far away for her to tell if one of them was Matt.

She hoped not.

Until that moment she'd assumed he would be somewhere nearby and she'd been counting on it. More than counting on it. She'd been eager to leave this room, to see him again.

But the thought that he might not be there—and the bitter wave of disappointment that washed through her along with it—told her just how eager she'd been.

Eager enough that it had been with him in mind that she'd chosen her sweater, she realized in a sudden flash of insight. Eager enough that it had been with him in mind that she'd shampooed her hair and left a few come-hither wisps to curl freely around her face and over the cut on her head to camouflage them. Eager enough that it had been with him in mind that she'd applied the makeup that made her look healthier. Eager enough that it had been with him in mind that she'd dabbed on a little of the perfume she'd found in her makeup bag.

But now she had to ask herself what in the world she'd been doing to actually be primping for a man in this, the worst of situations, when she should have been thinking only about how to straighten out what was going on with her.

But she knew the answer to that. And she closed her eyes and pressed her forehead to the frigid windowpane in disgust with herself.

She was just too attracted to the man.

At least the evening before she'd been able to convince herself that her attraction to him had been a result of her dazed state of mind.

But today she didn't have the same excuse.

No, she wasn't *completely* well. She did still have the knot on her head and her memory was just as messed up. But she wasn't as foggy-headed as she'd been and she just couldn't blame the attraction on that anymore.

The plain truth of it was that Matt McDermot was a nice, kind, pleasant, incredibly gorgeous, all-man man.

And she was attracted to him.

Who wouldn't be, after all? Handsome rescuer. Big, strong, considerate, caretaking cowboy. It wasn't much of a stretch to find him appealing since that was pretty powerful stuff.

But whether or not her weakness for him was understandable, Jenn knew she had to keep it under control. Because this was not the time nor the place to be looking for any kind of romance.

And she knew it.

She'd just have to bury the attraction the same way she'd buried the shaving kit filled with money in her suitcase so that neither Matt nor anyone else would know it existed.

She had more important things to deal with and she didn't need the complication of trying to start up a relationship on top of everything else.

But one thing was different—and better—today, she told herself as she opened her eyes and moved away from the window. She might be as attracted to Matt McDermot but she didn't have to be as vulnerable. She was more capable of resisting his allure now that her strength was back.

And resist it she would.

So, telling herself with conviction that it absolutely didn't matter where he was, she made her bed, dragged her suitcase into the closet where it was out of the way, and tidied the room so completely there wasn't a sign that she was in residence. Except for the teacup from the previous evening still on her bed table and she took that with her when she finally poked her nose out the bedroom door, intent on meeting head-on whatever or whoever was beyond it.

But whoever was beyond it was Matt, sitting on the hallway floor just outside her room, reading a newspaper.

"Mornin'," he said, looking up at her from his lower perch.

"Hi," Jenn returned, trying to keep the instant rise in her spirits from carrying her away and reminding herself that she was not—absolutely not—going to let her attraction to him have its way with her.

But that was easier said than done when she watched him push himself up the wall with the pure force of big cowboy-booted feet and thick-muscled legs that strained the denim of age-softened jeans until he was once more towering over her in magnificent masculinity.

"How's the patient today?" he asked, genuine concern wrinkling his squarish forehead above penetrating green eyes that seemed to take in every inch of her.

"I'm much better," she said a bit breathlessly, working to regain her equilibrium. "I'd say I was almost back to normal except that I still don't know what normal is."

"No return of the memory, huh?"

"Unfortunately not. I did have a dream that I was a very old woman, though, if that means anything."

"Probably your brain's perception of all those aches and pains you went to bed with last night."

"I hadn't thought of that," Jenn admitted, pleased with the interpretation and thinking that it made more sense than anything she'd come up with. It didn't explain why the dream had disturbed her, but then maybe feeling disturbed was just part and parcel of the present circumstances.

"How 'bout some breakfast? Are you hungry?" Matt asked then, interrupting her thoughts.

When Jenn focused on him again it was to find him making sure the tails of his heavy wool shirt were tucked in in back and then bending over to retrieve the newspaper from the floor.

The red shirt was worn over a white Henley T-shirt that peeked from behind his open collar and below the cuffs of his sleeves rolled to midforearm.

It made Jenn think of lumberjacks. The look suited the big man, though.

But then she couldn't come up with anything that wouldn't suit Matt. He was just so terrifically good-looking and well-built...

Breakfast. He'd asked if she wanted to eat, she reminded herself somewhat belatedly.

"I'm not all that hungry," she finally answered. "Maybe just a cup of tea." She held up her mug. "Besides, I was such a slugabed it's not long to lunchtime. No sense making a special mess for me, I'll just wait until then to eat."

"I wouldn't mind," he said so easily she believed him.

"Tea will be fine. Thanks anyway."

Matt nodded his head in the direction of the kitchen. "Let's make tea, then."

They went down the hall together and as they did, Jenn said, "The place is quiet. Is everybody gone?"

"The ladies got brave and thought they'd see if they could make it into town. My brothers are workin' out in the barn. Junebug—she runs things around the house—didn't make it in because of the snow, and Buzz is glued to the tube for *The Price Is Right* about now. So you're stuck with just me."

"Stuck" with him was not how she felt. She was glad to be alone with him, much as she knew she shouldn't be. But she wasn't going to say that.

Once they were in the kitchen, Matt took the cup out of her hand and pointed to the breakfast nook with his slightly but sexily dimpled chin.

"Sit while I make your tea," he ordered.

"I can do it. I'm really okay today. Well, except for the screws that are loose in my head." Loose screws that had her thinking more about him than about what she *should* be thinking about.

"Nope. You're a guest here and guests don't make their own tea," he decreed.

Since there didn't seem to be a point in arguing, Jenn opted for changing the subject. "Has there been any word from the sheriff or the radio station about me?"

Matt put a fresh cup filled with water into the microwave and turned it on.

"The phone lines were apparently fixed during the night because they're up and running again. I called the sheriff's office an hour or so ago. He said there's still been no response from the general public. He contacted the Cheyenne and Denver police early this morning, but you don't fit the description or the names in any of the missing persons cases."

Jenn just nodded, knowing it was probably par for the course for other police departments to be contacted by Elk Creek's sheriff but feeling uneasy with the thought of it anyway.

"So I guess that means you aren't a runaway," Matt concluded. "You aren't on anyone's wanted list and there doesn't seem to be any outstanding warrants for your arrest, so you must not be a criminal."

He added that as if it were a joke, but it wasn't funny to Jenn. The first thing that popped into her mind was the money in the shaving kit.

She told herself to take heart. If there weren't any

warrants out for her arrest it was because the money wasn't ill-gotten gains. Maybe it was just her savings.

But somehow that didn't put her mind to rest. It still seemed possible to her that if she'd taken the money illegally, it just hadn't been reported yet.

"Is there anything special or unusual for sale around here? Maybe I came to buy someone something for Christmas?" she said then, out of the blue. She'd wanted to broach that question more subtly but thoughts of all that cash and being on anyone's wanted list had somehow pushed the words out in hopes that she'd discover gift-buying was her purpose for having so much cash.

"Nothin' I know of," Matt answered without seeming to find the question noteworthy. "And I can't think of anything around these parts spectacular enough to come through a storm to buy."

He brought the tea to her when it was ready and set the cup on the table in front of where Jenn sat sideways on the bench seat so she was facing the center of the kitchen.

"I've been thinkin' 'bout how else to find out who you are, though, and figured we might try usin' the phone, see how far we get that way," he said. "We can check with the Denver directory assistance, see if there's a listing for you."

"That's a good idea," she agreed, even though it was a little disheartening to wonder if he already had a plan of action because he wanted to get rid of her. Especially when she'd been thinking a whole lot more about him and how great-looking he was and how much she wanted to be with him again than about how to figure out who she was.

Then, as if he could read her mind, he said, ''Not that I'm eager to have you get on your way to wherever you were headed. Even if we find out who you are or your memory comes back in the next ten minutes, your car is still buried and there's no tellin' when this storm will let up or when anyone can dig it out. So you're stuck with me for a while one way or another.''

Again with the stuck with him stuff. If only he knew how she really felt about that!

Jenn reminded herself of her determination to tamp down all her feelings about Matt and attend to business, so she stood, took her tea mug in hand and said, ''Let's get busy.''

''If you're not up to it we can hold off until tomorrow,'' he told her. ''You could have today to recuperate. There's no hurry.''

It almost seemed as if now that he'd made the suggestion he was stalling.

Jenn didn't know why that would be but didn't want to get her hopes up that it had any meaning beyond simple consideration for her health.

''I think I'm well enough to help make some phone calls,'' she assured him. Besides, the sooner she could find out the truth about herself, the sooner she could find out everything that was alarming her had no real reason to it.

Or that it did.

But she didn't want to think about that possibility

and so instead just said, "Where should we go for this?"

Matt studied her for a moment, as if to make sure she was genuinely well enough for what he'd proposed.

In the end he must have decided she was, because he said, "I thought the den would be good. One of us can use the regular phone and the other can use the cellular."

"Okay," Jenn agreed with a false cheerfulness when what she really felt was a deep hope that they didn't uncover something she'd be sorry for.

But she needn't have worried. They didn't uncover much of anything.

They gave the Denver operator Jenn's name and the address on her driver's license. When they were given a phone number to go with it, they thought they might have hit pay dirt and dialed it.

Only to hear a recording telling them that that number was no longer in service.

Since they couldn't go through the operator for every listing of a Johnson in the Denver directory, Matt called the Denver Public Library and persuaded someone there to fax them the pages from the local phone books with all the listings for Johnson.

While he and Jenn waited for the fax to come in, Jenn suggested they go through her purse again.

She'd done that the night before and hadn't found anything useful, but there didn't seem to be any harm in going through it again, in case Matt spotted something she'd missed.

He didn't. But it did occur to him to call the customer service number on her medical insurance card and her credit card and, while they were at it, to also try the number on the charge receipt for a gas station between Denver and Elk Creek on the off chance that it was a station she used often enough for them to know her.

So that was what they did.

Not that it made a whole lot of difference.

They didn't find out anything from the credit card or from the gas station where no one knew or recalled Jenn and responded as if they were pulling a prank. But the medical insurance company confirmed the address on her driver's license as the same one they had for her, informed her that she was covered on an individual policy, that she had no spouse or children listed on any of her forms, and that she'd marked the single box for marital status on her application.

As for releasing any information about claims that might have been paid to any doctor or hospital, the woman Jenn spoke to wouldn't tell her anything.

By then the fax came in. Eleven pages of Johnsons, two and a half of them with a first initial *J,* but not a Jenn in the lot. One of those listed with only the initial *J,* however, had the address on Jenn's driver's license and the number that directory assistance had already given them.

Just for the heck of it, they dialed the number one more time.

And one more time a recorded message said only that the number was no longer in service.

When lunchtime finally came around, Matt and Jenn ate sandwiches in the den while still making calls between mouthfuls to every Johnson on the eleven pages. Since Denver was also under the onslaught of the same blizzard hitting Elk Creek and had closed the schools and many of the businesses, they reached more than a fair share of people at home. But none of them knew a Jenn Johnson.

When a machine answered their calls, they left a message and the number at the ranch. When there was no answer, they marked the number on the faxed page to be retried later. All in all, it was a frustrating exercise.

"Supper's 'bout ready," Buzz called through the den's door after six that evening just as Matt and Jenn were hanging up their respective telephones.

"Thanks," Matt called to his grandfather. "We'll be out in a minute."

Then to Jenn he said, "I think it's about time to cry uncle on this deal anyway. But I have a friend in Denver. Maybe he'd go to the address on your license, see what he can find out."

"But if the phone is disconnected, don't you think that means there's no one there?"

Matt shrugged his broad shoulders. "You never know. Just because that particular number is out of service doesn't mean it wasn't replaced by a new number that's unlisted. Unlisted numbers aren't given out, but there could still be a working phone in the house. And people using it. Or maybe you sold the house. The new owners would have a different number that wouldn't be listed under your name so it wouldn't be given out as yours. But they might know who you are or be able to send us to the real estate agency that handled the sale and we could find out something through them."

"You're really good at this. Maybe you should be a private investigator," Jenn said with a small laugh, impressed by him.

But then so far she hadn't found anything about him that *didn't* impress her.

Matt chuckled at her half-joking suggestion. "Not a lot of call for P.I.s in Elk Creek. I'd starve."

"You could move to the big city."

He gave a mock shudder at the thought. "I'm a country boy. Cities give me claustrophobia. I like wide-open spaces and clean air and the smell of manure."

Jenn laughed. "The smell of manure?"

He grinned to let her know he'd been joking. "Well, maybe not the manure part. But I miss the rest whenever I have to be around too much concrete. Don't know that I'd like pokin' my nose into other people's business as a P.I., either. Window peepin' isn't my style. I like things up-front and out in the open. People, too."

I guess that leaves me out, she thought and for some reason it made her feel bad.

"I'd be up-front and open with you if I could, you know," she heard herself say before she realized she was going to.

"I'd hope so," he said. But he seemed uncomfortable with where the conversation had gone and he put some effort into getting them back to business. "Let me make this one last call to Bruce and then we can get out of this room. We've been in here so long I'm starting to feel as claustrophobic as I do in the city."

"We can't have that," Jenn agreed, pushing away the shadow of negativity that had settled over her moments before.

While Matt got a hold of his friend, Jenn stood up to stretch and, for the first time, took a good look around her.

The room was large and paneled in oak from floor to ceiling. Bookshelves lined one wall on either side of a rustic stone fireplace that gave the space a homier atmosphere. But there was definitely a male-enclave ambience to it all.

The furnishings had a masculine quality to them, too. Besides an overstuffed leather sofa against the wall opposite the fireplace there was a huge oak desk that monopolized the center of the room. Two high, leather wing chairs faced it, matching the desk chair behind it.

That was where Matt sat. Or rather, where he lounged at that moment, his feet propped on the corner of the desktop, his cowboy-booted feet crossed at the ankles.

At least that was where he was until his conversation with his friend was finished. Then he dragged his feet to the floor and stood to stretch much the way Jenn had moments before.

"Okay. He'll do it but he doesn't know when he'll be able to get through the snow to go. I told him there was no rush."

And for some reason that was music to Jenn's ears—both when she'd overheard him tell his friend on the phone and when he repeated it to her.

But she tamped down on the pleasure she felt at the prospect of staying longer in this big house with this big man, and firmly told herself she should be more unhappy with the fact that they were no closer to knowing much about her now than they had been before.

"Let's give this all a rest, have some supper and forget about it for today. What do you say?" Matt suggested.

"Sounds good to me," she agreed. Too good.

"Are you ready to meet the troops now?"

Jenn could hear the sounds coming from the kitchen that told her it was no small group she was about to encounter for the first time.

And even though she had a pretty good idea who she would be meeting when they left the seclusion of the den, she felt slightly daunted by the prospect.

But what else could she say, except, "Sure. Lead the way.

Matt didn't budge, though. Instead he shook his head and said, "Sorry, can't do that. My momma'd have my hide for showin' my backside to a lady."

Maybe his momma had been inclined to deprive ladies of the sight, Jenn thought.

But she knew Matt was only being a gentleman and so she went ahead of him through the door he'd opened for her.

As the sounds of voices and laughter and clattering dinner preparations became even louder, there was just one thing on her mind.

And it wasn't how many people she was about to be introduced to.

It was the fact that from here on she'd have to share Matt with the rest of his household.

And that she didn't want to.

Chapter Five

Unlike the night before, tonight the kitchen was full of people, all working together to produce a meal.

But even in the midst of so much commotion Jenn and Matt's entrance was noted. Everything stopped cold and the attention of eight people was suddenly aimed at Jenn.

"Better give 'er the roll call," Buzz told Matt after a round of hellos greeted them.

"I probably don't need to, do I?" Matt asked Jenn.

"Not really," Jenn admitted, yet again experiencing the phenomenon that left the people in the room strangers to whom she could pin names and facts.

"We've heard you can pull out information about folks like a rabbit from a hat."

Jenn focused on the woman who'd said that. She was about Jenn's size, extremely attractive, with the same golden-brown hair the men in the room had and pale green eyes that were similar, too, yet a shade that was all her own.

It would have been easy for anyone to see that she was related to the McDermot men, but Jenn could add to that.

"You're Kate, the only McDermot daughter and the youngest in the family. Well, the youngest of your generation of McDermots anyway. You just arrived in Elk Creek about a week ago. For Christmas. But it's a permanent move for you. You're going to stay and live on the ranch now."

Kate McDermot smiled. "One down, the rest to go," she said, encouraging what felt as much like a parlor trick to Jenn as it seemed to everyone else.

She and Matt went farther into the room, joining the group that stood at the business end of the kitchen while Buzz and two children waited at the breakfast nook.

One of Matt's brothers stood at the stove stirring what smelled like a pot of chili, and an identical-looking man was not far away with a stack of dinner plates held against his hip like a saddle.

"You two have to be Ry and Shane, the twins," Jenn said. "But I can't tell which of you is which."

They helped her out, Ry was stirring the chili and Shane was about to set the table.

Jenn nodded and filled in the blanks. "Shane was

named one of the World's Most Eligible Bachelors not long ago by *Prominence Magazine* but meeting Maya—'' Jenn scanned the faces of the remaining two women, settled on the one tearing lettuce into a big bowl and said ''—Maya remedied that in a hurry. Maya grew up in Elk Creek. Her mother is Margie Wilson of Margie Wilson's Café, the main restaurant in town. You're expecting a baby. I believe you just found out.''

''Wow!'' Maya said in a way that made Jenn wonder if she'd caused the other woman some embarrassment by mentioning the new pregnancy.

But then Maya added, ''You're more impressive than the psychics at the psychic fair I went to in Denver last year.''

She'd said that with a friendly tone in her voice, easing Jenn's apprehensions.

Then the third woman in the kitchen held up the knife she was using to slice a long loaf of bread and said, ''Now me,'' as if she were anxious for her turn.

''You're Tallie. You came to Elk Creek a while back to work as a nurse, midwife and physical therapist. You did Buzz's physical therapy after he broke his knee and that's how you met Ry. About the same time he inherited little Andrew over there.'' Jenn poked her chin toward the two-year-old who had lost interest in her and gone back to playing with a truck on the table of the breakfast nook, oblivious to what was going on with the adults. ''Tallie helped teach you what to do with a baby and one thing led to another. You got married not long before Bax and Carly did.''

"Ooo, ooo, do me, do me!"

Unlike the toddler, the little girl who had been with Buzz and Andrew at the breakfast nook had noticed what was going on and hopped off the bench seat to join in the fun.

Jenn couldn't help smiling at her. She wore a pair of pajama bottoms on her head and a full white slip pulled on over her clothes, the elastic waistband up around her chest but the hem still dragging on the floor.

"You're Evie Lee—"

"Evie Lee Lewis," the child corrected.

"She added the Lewis herself," Matt explained in an aside to Jenn.

"Evie Lee Lewis," Jenn amended. "You're Bax's daughter."

"And today I'm a bride, too."

"I can see that. And a beautiful one."

"Thank you," the child said as if the compliment were merely her due. "I came to stay with the old granddad 'cuz I'm not s'pose to be 'round germs for Christmas so I don't get sick."

"Sounds like a good idea."

"But what's your name?" Evie Lee demanded.

"I'm Jenn."

"I thought she couldn't 'member who she was," Evie Lee said as if someone had told her a fib and she'd caught them at it.

"I can't," Jenn said. "We just found out that's my name when we looked in my purse."

"Then how come you can 'member everything 'bout us? We don't even know you."

"Be nice, Evie Lee," Matt warned, putting a big hand on the child's shoulder to emphasize his reprimand.

"It's okay," Jenn assured. "Your question is a good one, Evie Lee, I just can't answer it. Something happened inside my head and now I can't remember anything about myself but I seem to know a lot about other people. People I've never met before. It's all pretty weird."

"I'll say. Is it magic?"

"Maybe," Jenn agreed with a laugh and without a better explanation.

Evie Lee seemed to accept that. She turned and went back to the breakfast nook where her Ken-doll groom waited.

"Well, welcome to Elk Creek, even if it isn't under the best of circumstances," Tallie said then.

"Thanks," Jenn answered, appreciating the response even as she hoped she was worthy of it.

"Tell you what I think," Shane said, since Jenn had named everyone in the room and finished with her exercise in trivia. "I think ol' Mattie here just brought you in to pull a good one on us all."

"Damn! Found out," Matt answered, playing along with his older brother's teasing. "I had to pay extra for the knot on her head, too, and it didn't even fool you."

"It's a trick?" Evie Lee asked from the breakfast nook, obviously still listening.

"Your uncle Shane is only kidding," Maya assured the child.

Evie Lee still looked suspicious but in the end she

slapped the heel of one hand against her forehead and said, "I don't know what's goin' on."

Seeing the action, Andrew copied her, bouncing his palm off his head and saying, "Dunno what's goin' on."

The whole room erupted in laughter and when it died down, Ry said, "Soup's on," and everyone went back into motion.

Even Jenn and Matt were assigned tasks—to fill glasses with water and ice.

As they did, Matt leaned in very close to Jenn—close enough so that his breath was a warm cloud against her ear—and said, "Don't mind Shane's teasin'. He was just giving me a hard time. He doesn't doubt that you've lost your memory."

"I figured as much," Jenn whispered back, grateful for the reassurance anyway.

She was also glad to be included in the dinner preparations—no matter how minor the job—because it meant she was being treated like one of the family. Something that continued as conversation turned to everyday things like when they were all going out to cut down the Christmas tree and how preparations for their Christmas Eve party were coming.

It was nice for Jenn.

She didn't have any idea what kind of family she'd come from—if it had been big or small, or if she'd had any at all—but she found being a part of this warm, friendly group very satisfying. She decided that if she had to share Matt, these were good people to do it with.

As the meal and the evening wore on, there was a lot of teasing and joking among the brothers and Kate, a lot of communal caring for the two children and the elderly man, a lot of compassion for Jenn and how odd things were for her. But still and all, no matter how pleasant were the hours that passed in eating and cleanup and conversation, and regardless of the fact that Matt was never far from her side, what was uppermost in Jenn's mind was getting back to the one-on-one with him.

So when the kids were shuffled off to bed and suggestions were being made for movie-watching or board games, Jenn was only too happy to have Matt lean in close to her ear once more and say, "Are you up for a short walk in the snow, by any chance? I have cabin fever somethin' fierce."

"A walk sounds good to me," she answered quietly, trying to force her heart not to beat so merrily at the prospect.

"Great. What do you have in the way of warm clothes and boots?"

"Mostly just what you found me in yesterday. Except that there are some gloves, earmuffs and a scarf in my suitcase."

"That stuff is good, but your coat and shoes from yesterday aren't."

Matt turned to the room in general and announced that he and Jenn were going to get some fresh air but that Jenn needed some snow boots.

She couldn't tell them what size shoe she wore until she removed one from her foot to check. Maya produced a pair of heavily insulated boots she told Jenn she could keep.

"How about a coat?" Kate asked.

"I'll give her one of mine," Matt answered as he ushered Jenn out of the kitchen and back down the hallway that took them to their rooms.

"Change your shoes and get those gloves and things. I'll grab the coats and meet you in your room in ten minutes," Matt instructed when they were outside their respective doors, just before disappearing through his own.

True to his word, Matt knocked on her door ten minutes later. By then Jenn had pulled on an extra pair of socks and Maya's boots, wrapped a black knit muffler around her neck and, with matching gloves in hand, was ready to let him in.

He wore the big fleece-lined suede coat he'd had on the day before, buttoned all the way up the front, and the same cowboy hat he'd worn then, too.

He was carrying a jacket that was similar to the one he wore, only slightly smaller and shorter in length.

"I ordered this from a catalog before the cold weather hit. It was too small but I never got around to sendin' it back. It'll still be big for you but it should keep you plenty warm."

He held it for her to slip into and she did, nearly getting lost in it because while it may have been too small for Matt, it was still much, much too large for Jenn.

So large it made her laugh when he settled it over her shoulders.

"Are you in there?" he said as if calling down a deep well.

"I think so," she called back the same way.

"Would you rather I see if Kate or one of my sisters-in-law has something more your size?"

"No, that's okay. This is nice and warm." Jenn declined the offer mainly because the coat smelled like Matt. A masculine, citrusy scent that it must have picked up hanging in his closet. The scent enveloped her as surely as the fleecy lining, and she liked it too much to want to give it up.

So instead she snuggled into the jacket's depths and buttoned the front before he could change his mind about lending it to her.

Then she put on her earmuffs and gloves while Matt took a pair of leather gloves of his own out of his pocket and did likewise.

"All set?" he asked when he had.

"All set."

"Now don't push this. As soon as you feel tired or cold, let me know and we'll come back in and call it a night so you can get some rest."

"I will," she promised, although at that moment she felt too exhilarated to imagine herself in any hurry to end the evening.

They went outside through the French doors from her rooms, stepping into a whipped cream world sprinkled with glitter. There was no wind so everything was still and silent and peaceful. And so, so beautiful.

"It's funny," Jenn said as they started off, heading down the tire tracks that had compressed the snow from the main road along the side of the house to the garage around back. "I just had this feeling that if I weren't here with you and your family I'd be all alone and this storm wouldn't seem so nice."

"A flash of memory?"

"Not really. Only a sense."

"Of loneliness?"

"I guess so. And isolation."

"Sounds bad," Matt said, but in such a comical way it shot the statement with humor. "'Round here you have to fight for time by yourself. Even with all the separate suites designed for privacy."

"Do you need a lot of it? Time by yourself, I mean."

He shrugged his shoulders as he flipped the collar of his coat up so that it brushed his sharp jawline. "I wouldn't say I need a lot of time alone, no. But every now and then…"

"You just need to be away from everything and everyone?"

"Guess that makes me the loner of the family."

"I wouldn't have guessed that about you," Jenn said, stealing a glance at his profile and enjoying the rugged, masculine sight thrown into relief against all the white around them.

"Are you actually telling me there's something you don't know about me?" he teased.

"Maybe one or two things."

"Mmm. And what else *do* you know about me?" he asked then, giving her a sideways look.

"Let's see. I know you were born and raised in Texas. That's where your father lived and where your mother ended up after eloping with him. I know you went to college there and got a degree. But now that I think about it, I don't know in what.''

''Agriculture,'' he supplied.

''Ah. I know you worked the family ranch after you graduated, but when your folks decided to retire and travel, you opted not to stay and take over that place but to come up here and work this one with your brothers. That must mean you aren't *too* much of a loner.''

Matt chuckled and it was a rich sound that seemed to dance on the frigid night air. ''You've got me there.''

''I also know you're single, have no kids anywhere anyone knows about, and that's it.''

''I don't have any kids anywhere anyone *doesn't* know about, either,'' he assured her.

''Good,'' she said, laughing at him. Then, as if he could perform the same trick she could, she said, ''Okay, now you tell me about me.''

''Let's see.'' He tipped his chin up toward the overcast sky and closed his eyes as if he were divining his answer. ''You're single, too, and have no kids—''

''Too easy. You found that out from my medical insurance,'' she said as if she really did expect him to tell her something she didn't know.

''Your livelihood must not depend on the telephone because you've either had it turned off or keep your number a closely guarded secret.''

''Me and Greta Garbo.''

''And you're probably self-employed.''

"Again, from the medical insurance policy. Although I could be *un*employed."

"And independently wealthy. You're probably a rich heiress who's run off to mingle with the common folk so she can see how the other half lives."

"That's it!" she said as if he'd hit the jackpot. "Except if I'm an heiress, how come as we speak there's a very large hole in the heel of the second pair of socks I put on tonight?"

"Maybe because you're the original holey-sock heiress?"

"Ah, of course."

They'd reached the main road by then and turned to go back toward the house.

Even in the distance it was an impressive sight— the big house all lit up with Christmas lights aglow in the darkness, more of the tiny white lights strung around the branches of the tree that canopied the roof.

"If this is mingling with the common folk to see how the other half lives, I'm not sure I'm getting the real picture," she said.

Besides the lavishness of his home and property, there was also nothing common about Matt—something she would rather not have been so aware of.

"So, is it just my family you know so much about or all of Elk Creek? And the rest of the world, too?" he asked.

Jenn thought about that, mentally picking through what she could recall. "Seems like I know a lot about Elk Creek and the people in it, but that's the limit. I couldn't tell you where in Denver the address on my driver's license is or anything about anyone there. And nothing springs to mind about anywhere else, either. But I seem to have an encyclopedic knowledge of Elk Creek and its citizens—not merely the McDermots.''

''Elk Creek isn't in the encyclopedia.''

''Maybe I was beamed up by aliens who drained my memory banks, replaced them with nothing but knowledge of the place I was closest to when they took me and then beamed me back down.''

''Any memories of little green men?''

''Sorry. They must have cleared that, too.'' Then Jenn sobered somewhat as a thought she'd been having off and on during the last twenty-four hours came to mind again. ''What if I don't get my memory back and no one ever comes looking for me?''

She regretted the apprehension that echoed in her voice but she hadn't been able to keep it out.

Matt looked at her again, for a long while this time, through eyes that chased away the chill of the night air for Jenn.

''I think we'll find out everything we need to know about you eventually,'' he said with a calm confidence that eased her fears. ''We'll keep looking and turn something up, or your memory will come back. But one way or another, everything will work out. Worse comes to worst, you'll stay here in Elk Creek and we'll all get to know the new you as well as you know us.''

Somehow that didn't seem like such a horrible prospect—staying in Elk Creek, being close to Matt, getting to know more than a few surface things about him...

"Maybe we will find out I'm an heiress," she said in a hurry to keep her thoughts from straying too far in Matt's direction.

They'd returned to the house by then and the overly cheery note in her voice must have alerted Matt to the anxiousness that was still lying just below the surface. Because as they climbed the porch steps and followed the painted wood floor around the house toward the door to her rooms, he reached over and slipped one of her earmuffs off so he could lean in and speak into her ear the way he had in the kitchen earlier.

"Everything will be all right," he said in a voice for her alone. "I'll make sure of it."

She believed he could, too. At that moment, anyway. She believed he was powerful enough to make certain everything would work out.

But then he didn't know about all that money in her suitcase...

Still, Jenn opted for a return to their joking as an escape from thoughts she didn't want to have—thoughts about the situation and about the warm lava that he'd just sent bubbling through her veins. "Aliens. I'm pretty sure this whole thing can be blamed on aliens."

"I guess that makes you a gift from heaven."

"Or the booby prize."

Poor choice of phrases. It sounded too lewd to Jenn.

It also made her think too much about that particular portion of her own anatomy—breasts that seemed to stand up and take notice every time she got anywhere around Matt.

But at least the porch light and the Christmas lights didn't glow bright enough for him to see her face coloring.

Although, since they'd arrived at the door to her rooms she knew that if they both went inside he'd be able to see it then.

So she acted as if he'd just walked her to the door of an apartment after a date, turned her back to it and faced him.

"Well, thanks for a lovely evening," she joked.

"Sure. Anytime," he countered the same way. "Will I be able to see you again?"

"I'll have to check my calendar. I'm a pretty busy person, you know."

"I know but I was hopin' to get you into town tomorrow to do a little shoppin' with me, maybe see if anybody recognizes you. Any chance you can work me in?"

Ooh, what came to mind in terms of working him in....

Dangerous images...

Jenn grappled with them to subdue them and when she finally had, she pretended pique and said, "You want to put me on display like a trophy wife, is that it?"

He smiled a wicked smile. "I wouldn't mind showin' you off," he admitted, still playing along but with a new hint of flirtation.

"I suppose I can rearrange my plans," she conceded.

"And tomorrow night everybody's goin' ice skating. Think you're up to that? We're diggin' out the old horse-drawn sleigh and taking that to the lake. I can promise hot chocolate and spiced cider and roasted marshmallows, if that helps persuade you."

"That is pretty persuasive." Along with the idea of a sleigh ride and an evening of ice skating with him. "I suppose I'll just have to clear my whole schedule for you."

Once more he leaned in to whisper, "I'll make it worth your while."

The warm gust of his breath along with the innuendo in his tone were all it took for happy, sensuous things to skitter through her.

Only this time—unlike any of those that had come before—instead of straightening up from leaning down to talk into her ear, he moved just enough so that his face was close to hers, his dark green eyes delving into her eyes in a way they never had before.

Jenn stared back into those penetrating spruce-colored depths, held by them as surely as if they were an embrace.

She could have sworn Matt was going to kiss her.

The culmination of the day and evening spent close together, the culmination of this walk in the wonderland of Christmas snow and all the teasing and joking and fun they'd had, would be a kiss.

She waited for a kiss from supple male lips that she'd bet anything would know just what they were doing and how to do it to such perfection that it would leave her even more weak-kneed than she already was just from imagining it.

But that wasn't what he did.

At the very moment when she thought he was drawing closer, when she thought she was right on the verge of having his mouth pressed to hers just the way she wanted it to be, he pulled back.

Way back.

Even stepping to the porch's railing to put an extra distance between them.

"You'd better go in and get out of this cold," he said, nodding at her door.

"Aren't you coming?" she asked, wanting him to, now that her blush had passed and his *not* going in with her meant the end of her time with him.

"Nah, I think I better check a few things in the barn while I'm out here. Make sure the horses are all bedded down."

Jenn just nodded, knowing he was making that up to avoid coming in with her.

But then that was probably for the best, she reasoned. They didn't have any business kissing, after all.

Except that once they'd said their good-nights and Matt had watched her go inside, Jenn didn't feel a whole lot better because they'd stayed on the straight and narrow.

She felt like a woman who'd been waiting to be kissed—a woman who had wanted *badly* to be kissed—and not gotten her wish.

And regardless of how much she told herself it was for the best, that just wasn't how it seemed.

Chapter Six

Matt was up and outside again early the next morning. It was long past his turn to shovel snow and so that was what he was doing.

Well, that and thinking about Jenn.

But then thinking about Jenn was all he ever seemed to do these days. Nothing else occupied his thoughts quite the same way. In fact, even when he tried to concentrate on something else he couldn't. Before he knew it, there she'd be instead, complete with vivid images of those twilight-blue eyes, that paprika-red hair, those delicately beautiful features, that damnably enticing little body....

He was like a man obsessed.

And he didn't appreciate it.

Beautiful features and a damnably enticing body

were not what he was supposed to be thinking about. He was supposed to be thinking about how to jog Jenn's memory or find out who she was and where she belonged. He was supposed to be tending to business.

But tending to business was what he was having trouble concentrating on.

And the worst part of it was that he knew better. He knew that he was out of his mind to be having the kinds of thoughts he was having about her. To be enjoying her company so much. To be losing himself in fantasies where being snowbound with her was only the beginning.

Wasn't he ever going to learn? he demanded of himself as harshly as he would of someone doing something reckless and frivolous and completely irrational.

How much did it take for him to wise up?

There were just too many unanswered questions about Jenn, and nobody was more aware than Matt that what he didn't know could hurt him.

A whole hell of a lot.

So back off, he silently commanded as he hoisted shovelfuls of fluffy white snow onto piles that were nearly chest high already.

Backing off was sound advice and he knew it.

Okay, maybe she didn't have a husband out there somewhere waiting for her. Or kids. But that didn't mean she was a free agent. She could have a boyfriend. A significant other. A fiancé who hadn't given her a ring yet.

Of course none of those things were as binding as a husband or kids, but still...

The bottom line was that he just didn't know the kinds of things he needed to know about her. The kinds of things that could crop up and bite him in the behind when he least expected it. When he was in over his head with her. She was a mystery. A complete enigma. And because of that, she was also the last person on the face of the earth he should be letting himself be susceptible to. The last person on the face of the earth he should be nearly kissing.

But damn if resisting his attraction to her and everything it was doing to him wasn't easier said than done.

It wasn't as if he were *choosing* to have her take up residence in his mind as surely as she'd taken it up in his house. It wasn't as if he *wanted* to be itching to see her, to be champing at the bit to be with her every minute. It wasn't as if he were *glad* to be dreaming dreams about her coming into his room in the middle of the night with soft light illuminating her from behind so that he could see the silhouette of her naked body through some diaphanous nightgown. It wasn't as if he were happy to wake up in a cold sweat of desire that he knew had no business entering the picture at all.

"Hey! You have a grudge against that snow out there?"

The sound of Ry's voice calling from the house made Matt realize just how much of a vengeance he'd been putting into jamming the shovel into the drifts and throwing the snow to the side of the walkways he was clearing.

"Just tryin' to get it done," Matt called back as if there wasn't a thing out of the ordinary in his vigor.

"Uh-huh," Ry said loud enough for Matt to hear. "Well, coffee's ready and looks like you're 'bout done out there. Why don't you come in and I'll pour you a cup?"

"Be right there," Matt assured, noticing only then that his racing thoughts had made quick work of his snow shoveling.

When he'd cleared the last two shovelfuls he stomped his booted feet back to the porch to clear them of snow, propped the shovel against the house to wait for its next use and went inside.

He pulled off his gloves and stowed them in his coat pocket, then left his hat and coat hanging on the hall tree to dry.

Free of his winter gear, he ran his hands through his hair to rough it up—and maybe in hopes that it might clear his head of the lingering thoughts of Jenn and all he shouldn't be doing in regards to her.

But it hardly helped. Instead, on the way to the kitchen, he found himself wondering how long it would be before she woke up and they could start the day together.

No, maybe he didn't ever learn.

Ry was the only one in the kitchen when Matt got there. Ry and the smell of fresh brewed coffee. It was too early for anybody else yet since daylight was hardly half an hour old.

Ry nodded silently to the steaming mug in front of the coffeepot not far from where he stood.

Matt picked up the cup, mumbled his thanks and warmed his hands around it before taking a cautious sip.

"What are you doin'?" Matt asked his brother with a nod of his own at the tray on which Ry was placing napkins, plates and silverware.

"Tallie's off work this week and sleepin' in. Thought I'd make her breakfast."

"You?" Matt said incredulously to goad his brother. "You're serving someone breakfast in bed?"

Ry smiled a smug smile. "You bet," he said, infusing those two simple words with his ulterior motive.

"Lookin' for an excuse to wake her up, aren't you?" Matt surmised.

Ry just smiled and changed the subject. "Sheriff called. I picked it up right away so the phone didn't rouse the whole house."

Matt raised his eyebrows and fought a feeling of dread at what a call from the sheriff at this early hour might mean. "He found out who Jenn is and somebody's comin' for her," Matt guessed, voicing what was the cause of that feeling.

Ry gave him a sideways glance that was full of suspicion. "Why do I think you might be barricadin' the doors if I say yes?"

"Fertile imagination?"

"I don't think so. But no, that's not what the sheriff had to say. Said he's havin' trouble gettin' any

answers to any questions he puts out about her—
beyond that she's not on any missing persons reports
or wanted lists. Said not to expect much help findin'
out who she is until after Christmas. Maybe after
New Year's. And that he's goin' away himself today
and forgot to tell you, which is why he called so
early. He's packin' into the high country for the next
two weeks to a cabin he has up there. Said that you
can contact his deputy if you need to, but otherwise
you're pretty much on your own with Jenn for the
time being.''

Ry cast Matt another glance and Matt knew his
brother was looking for his reaction to that last bit
of news.

For Matt's part, he was trying like crazy not to
let his pleasure in that show.

But he was definitely *feeling* plenty of it.

More than he knew he should be feeling.

"In other words, get used to having her around
because she's apt to be here for a while," Matt said,
hoping to sound as if that were a nuisance, and fail-
ing enough to make his brother chuckle at him.

"Yeah, I knew that'd break your heart," Ry said
facetiously.

Matt just sipped his coffee.

"She must be pretty unattached if nobody's
lookin' for her," Ry observed.

"Or she's runnin' from something," Matt said,
playing devil's advocate more than anything else.

"You think she's runnin' from the law?"

Matt laughed at that notion. "Jenn? No. But

maybe she's runnin' away from somebody or something.''

"Such as?''

Matt shrugged. "An abusive boyfriend. A harassing boss. A stalker. A broken heart. But that's the point, isn't it? I don't know for sure who she is or what she's comin' from.''

"A dash of mystery'll keep you interested.''

"Or burn me,'' Matt said wryly.

"Sarah,'' Ry said, studying Matt from beneath a sudden frown.

"Sarah,'' Matt confirmed.

"Jenn seems nice enough,'' Ry said then, in a way that sounded like an attempt to look on the bright side.

But Matt couldn't go along with it, much as he might be inclined to. "People aren't always what they seem.''

"Some of 'em are.''

"You tryin' to talk me into something?''

"Just sayin' sometimes you have to trust people. Take 'em at face value. You don't do that much anymore.''

"Because sometimes being too trusting of people is just plain stupid.''

"Jeez, when'd you get so cynical, little brother?''

"When did you get so soft?''

"Soft is sure as shootin' *not* how I'm spendin' a lot of time these days,'' Ry countered with a randy smile and a full load of insinuation in his voice.

"Yeah, well, you had it easy with Tallie. She came complete with a town full of people who knew her and everything about her. Not much to worry about in that case. She couldn't have kept a secret if she'd wanted to.''

"So because you don't have a world of prior knowledge about Jenn, you're gonna keep her at arm's length. Even if it kills you. Is that what you're tellin' me?''

"Yep."

"Good luck."

"What makes you think I need it?''

Ry glanced Matt's way a third time, his expression letting Matt know he'd seen right through him. "She's in your blood already.''

"Think so, huh?'' Matt said, trying to play it cool.

"Yes siree. But go ahead and put some effort into that keepin'-her-at-arm's-length thing. Ought to be fun to watch.''

Matt knew Ry was only countering his earlier goad with one of his own. And if they'd still been boys, one or the other of them would have pounced in response and they'd both have ended up with bruises and black eyes before it was over.

But they were older and wiser now, so all Matt did was roll his eyes as if Ry were too far out in left field to be taken seriously.

And all Ry did was laugh, pick up the tray that now held sweet rolls, fresh fruit, cream, sugar and two cups of coffee.

"Yep, be fun to watch this one,'' Ry said as he left Matt alone in the kitchen.

But Matt had too much on his mind to care that he was amusing his older brother.

He just kept thinking about Jenn being around for some time to come and how that possibility suddenly brightened his Christmas spirits about ten thousand watts.

Oh, yeah, keeping her at arm's length was going to be quite a project. Especially when he kept picturing a literal version of it in his mind. Arm's length wasn't all that much distance between them.

It wouldn't take more than a simple bend of the elbow to bring her in a whole lot closer. Close enough to do what he'd almost done the night before. What he'd wanted to do so damn bad it had nearly hurt not to do it.

One bend of the elbow and keeping her at arm's length could turn into kissing her.

And then he'd *really* be in trouble.

Even with Matt's truck in four-wheel-drive and chains on the tires it was a slow-go from the ranch into town after lunch that day.

Jenn didn't mind, though. The heater kept the cab warm; there were continuous Christmas carols playing on the radio; the air was redolent with the scent of Matt's aftershave; she was bundled up in her black leggings, a funnel-neck sweater and the coat Matt had given her the previous evening; and everything worked together to make a cozy atmosphere despite the fact that they were slowly wending their way through more snow than Jenn could ever remember seeing.

It also didn't hurt that she was with Matt. Or that he'd told her that unless someone in town recognized her or she had a spontaneous return of her memory that gave them a clue as to where she was supposed to be, she was likely to spend at least the next two weeks with him.

Of course she knew she shouldn't be heartened by that news. But when everything was stripped down to the bare bones, the truth was that she was secretly happy with the prospect of spending an extended time in his company.

She just had to keep things under control, she vowed yet again. She just had to not let that attraction to him carry her away. She had to make sure their relationship stayed well within the boundaries of propriety and that nothing made them venture beyond those boundaries.

The way her thoughts kept doing.

Especially the night before when she'd thought he was going to kiss her.

But he hadn't kissed her. And that was good. Even if it hadn't felt good at the time.

Because kissing would definitely be stepping beyond those boundaries.

So no kissing, she swore. No nothing except two people passing time together in a perfectly friendly manner that never goes outside the realm of simple courtesy and friendliness.

And she meant it, too. She really did.

Until they reached Elk Creek and Matt came around to her side of the truck to help her down, taking her hand so she didn't slip on the ice on the truck's side runners.

Just as that slight physical contact had sent her

into a tailspin before, it did again, weakening her knees and all her vows in an instant.

Two people passing time together in a perfectly friendly manner that never goes outside the realm of innocent friendliness...

She recited that vow to herself over and over again as if to permanently ingrain it in her mind.

Then he let go of her hand and Jenn breathed once more, convinced she'd made some headway in keeping things between them on the friendship level.

"First stop, Bax's office so he can check you over again," Matt announced as he closed the truck's door behind them.

It took Jenn a moment to reset her thoughts and focus, and realize Matt was talking to her. But when she finally did she also took in the fact that she was standing on the snowpacked sidewalk in front of the three-storey redbrick building where she'd awakened on Tuesday after Matt had rescued her.

"The Molner Mansion," she said, peering up at the tall building and seizing the safety of another morsel of trivia that popped into her head. "Built by one of the founding families of Elk Creek as their home, and later donated to the town and turned into the medical facility. There's a dentist's office but the rest of the building is taken up by the doctor's office and examining rooms, an emergency center, outpatient surgical facilities and two hospital rooms for when someone needs to stay over because they can't get to the regular hospital in Cheyenne."

"I didn't know the history of the building," Matt

admitted as he ushered Jenn inside. "Maybe you could have a future here as a tour guide."

The office was bustling, but Matt and Jenn received preferential treatment and were taken back immediately by Carly, who was acting as assistant to her husband in the absence of Tallie, the town nurse.

"That works out," Jenn observed when Carly explained what she was doing. "You teach school— junior high geography—and since there aren't any classes until after the first of the year you're free."

"And this way I get to see more of my big love muffin, even though he's so busy," Carly finished for her, teasing her husband with the silly endearment at the same time.

"Big love muffin?" Matt repeated to his brother who was looking into Jenn's eyes with a lighted ophthalmoscope.

"It's my required title around the office," Bax answered without embarrassment, winking at Jenn when he'd taken the ophthalmoscope away.

Then he said, "How's the memory? Anything coming back yet?"

Jenn shook her head. "Nothing. I feel fine, but my head is still in such a thick fog I can't get through it."

"She's still churning out information about us and Elk Creek, though," Matt contributed. "She just gave me a history lesson about this building."

"The old Molner Mansion," Carly confirmed. "Maybe that's what you are—a history teacher or an historian of some kind."

"An historian of small towns?" Matt said. "Is there such a thing?"

No one knew but the general consensus was that it wasn't likely.

"Besides," Matt added, "don't get me wrong— I'm fond of this little town, but it's hardly one for the history books, is it?"

Carly admitted that it wasn't.

"It doesn't look like the authorities are going to be much help in figuring out who I am for a while, either," Jenn said. "At least not until after the holidays."

Matt explained to his brother and sister-in-law what he'd told Jenn earlier about the sheriff's phone call.

"Well, at least you're in good hands," Bax concluded with a raise of his chin in Matt's direction.

The mere mention of those hands sent a little skitter up Jenn's spine that she tried to ignore and instead said, "I was just lucky that it was Matt who found me."

"Lucky or fated," Carly said, sharing a glance with her husband that made him smile.

There was suddenly an air of intimacy between the doctor and his wife, and Jenn felt as if she and Matt were somehow intruding.

Matt must have felt the same thing because he stepped in and said, "If you're done here, we need to do some Christmas shopping."

That seemed to break the spell that had woven around the other couple and Bax said, "I thought you already had my Porsche bought."

Matt played along with his brother's jest. "I have to have it wrapped, though."

Bax confirmed that Jenn was doing fine—with the exception of her diminished memory—and on their way out of the office Matt reminded his brother about the plans for ice skating that evening and let him know Evie Lee was enjoying her stay at the ranch. Before Jenn knew it, she and Matt were back out in the winter weather heading for his truck again.

Center Street, which was Elk Creek's main drag, formed a keyhole around the town square at the north end where the medical facility was. Keeping the old Molner Mansion company was the local school, the courthouse, the church, and several other establishments that wouldn't do them any good for Christmas shopping. So Matt drove to the other end of the wide avenue where quaint, old-fashioned, multilevel buildings lined each side.

Jenn took a long look around her as Matt parked nose-first near the General Store. Center Street looked like a picture off a Christmas card.

Each store was decorated with its own touch in lights around windows and along eaves, wreaths on doors, and trees and Christmas displays adorning storefronts.

The tall Victorian streetlights that bordered Center Street were all wound with evergreen boughs and red ribbons tied into bows just below their lamps, and from high up, strung between the tops of the tallest buildings, more boughs and ribbons were hung like smiles from one to the other.

All in all it was a beautiful sight, and although

none of it was familiar to Jenn, she still felt right at home.

"Oh, this is so nice," she said more to herself than to Matt when they were both out of the truck and headed for the General Store.

"It does look pretty good, doesn't it?" Matt agreed with a touch of pride.

In deference to the snow there weren't many vehicles parked along the sides of the road, but still there were a lot of people milling around from shop to shop—the advantage of a small community where most things were within walking distance.

The General Store in particular was busy but it just seemed to add to the Christmas spirit to have so many people looking over the wares, chatting and laughing and wishing each other happy holidays.

The air inside was warm and smelled of the spiced tea steeping in a pot on an overturned pickle barrel for the customers to sample, while the carols Matt and Jenn had been listening to on the radio were playing as background music there, too.

Word traveled fast in a small town and apparently news of Jenn had been the most recent topic because as she and Matt browsed, everyone they encountered stopped to be introduced to her, conveyed their hopes that she would regain her memory before too long. Then they invariably wanted to know what she could tell them about themselves.

There were a few disappointed souls about whom Jenn drew a blank, but for the most part she could come up with a tidbit or two about everyone.

She made a particular point of asking to see the

new babies of the two sisters who were juggling the running of the store with caring for the infants behind the counter—Kansas Heller and her sister Della.

Della's daughter was six months old and her fifth child. Jenn knew Della had four older kids by her late first husband and now this baby with her second, Yance Culhane.

Kansas also had a six-month-old daughter, but she and her husband Linc Heller, had adopted the baby because Kansas was unable to have kids.

"And Danny, there's also Danny, isn't there?" Jenn asked, recalling that Kansas was also mother to her husband's four-year-old son.

At the sound of his name the little guy came running from somewhere in the rear of the store, but once he realized there were only unexciting adults to meet, he disappeared again.

The General Store wasn't the only place Jenn was treated like a visiting celebrity.

Everywhere she and Matt went that afternoon they were waylaid by folks eager to meet her and be told what she knew about them. It was fun for Jenn and it gave her a chance to talk to a lot of people.

But the experience was like visiting one of her own dreams. She recognized faces and put names with them, the whole time realizing she didn't really know them. And they certainly didn't know her. No one had a clue who she was.

And yet all of Elk Creek was warm and welcoming anyway, and she felt embraced by the whole town by the time Matt had finished his shopping and they returned to his truck.

It was just that packages were all they took with them, because they hadn't learned one whit more about Jenn than they'd known before.

There was a message waiting for Matt when he and Jenn arrived home, a message to call his friend Bruce in Denver. So once they'd both taken off their coats, they went into the den to return the call.

Jenn couldn't tell much from Matt's side of the conversation, nor could she really tell what she felt as she waited.

What if this was it? she thought. What if Matt's friend had found out who she was and was telling Matt to put her on the next train to Denver, back to her family or friends? Back to her real life? How would she feel about that?

Maybe not so good, she decided.

Definitely not as good as she had felt this morning when it had seemed that she was going to have to stay here with Matt at least through the holidays.

Because after yet another day with him, teasing her, talking to her, taking care of her, the idea of leaving him behind was all the more hard to swallow.

Not a good thing, she knew. But there it was. Spending time with him was more important to her than finding herself.

By the time he finally hung up the phone, she was holding her breath in wary anticipation of what he was going to relay to her and wondering why everyone in Elk Creek got such a kick out of a stranger being able to tell them things about themselves. Because at that moment she wasn't so eager to have the same thing happen to her.

"Well," Matt began. "Bruce managed to get out on the roads today. He went to the address on your driver's license."

"And?" Jenn prompted when it seemed that Matt was taking his sweet time about going on.

"The address is in a suburban area outside Denver where the houses were all bought by the city and leveled to build a shopping center."

Which meant no one was asking for her to be sent back to them.

Jenn breathed again, a long, slow exhale that let her tense shoulders relax.

"So that was a dead end," Matt concluded. Although he didn't sound any more disappointed than she felt.

In fact, not only *didn't* she feel disappointed, but it occurred to her that if she'd owned one of the houses the city had bought, that might account for the $2,157 in her suitcase. Of course that wasn't much of a profit for the sale of an entire house but still that thought was preferable to thinking she'd come by the money in some less acceptable way. Although she still didn't feel confident enough about the likelihood to let Matt know she had all that cash.

What she did say, though, was, "Maybe when the city took over and I had to move anyway, I just decided to move to Elk Creek."

"Maybe. Although why Elk Creek of all places, since you don't seem to have a connection here?"

Good question.

"Maybe I just picked it at random, because I don't have any ties anywhere else. You know, like I opened a map, closed my eyes, pointed a finger and wherever it landed was where I was going."

"Okay," Matt said as if it were possible, but he wasn't ruling out any other possibilities, either. "But that still doesn't explain how you know so much about everything and everybody here."

"Research?"

"Research," he repeated as if trying it on for size. "I suppose that's possible, too, but I don't know what kind of research would turn up the stuff you seem to know. You have an insider's track. And the bottom line is, here we are, still not knowing any more than we did before."

That seemed to have some importance to him and even though Jenn wasn't sure why, she felt inclined to say, "I'm sorry."

"For what?"

She shrugged. "Everything. You did a simple good deed and here you are, with nothing for your reward but a dingbat for a houseguest and a lot of frustration."

Matt chuckled to himself, closed his eyes and shook his head as if she couldn't be more off base in what she was assuming.

Then he opened those gorgeous green eyes again and grinned at her. "Dingbat?"

"I don't know what else you'd call me. Except maybe some things that aren't as kind."

"I don't think you're a dingbat. And I'm afraid what I'm feeling isn't frustration. Well, not the kind you're thinking about, anyway."

She wanted to ask what kind of frustration he *was* feeling but she couldn't bring herself to. It sounded personal and she didn't think she had any business prying into it.

Besides, she had the sense that it was better that she didn't know. Better that things between them stay within those boundaries she'd told herself earlier to abide by.

Matt let his head fall forward and rubbed the back of his neck with one big hand, as if massaging the stress away.

Frustration and stress—not effects she was glad to cause.

It crossed her mind to go to him from where she stood on the opposite side of the desk and do some massaging of her own to help out.

But as quick as the urge struck she pushed it away, holding her ground. Although not without difficulty as she drank in the sight of Matt dressed in tight jeans and a red flannel shirt stretched to its limits across mile-wide shoulders.

"I think I probably ought to do a little more snow shoveling," he said then, out of the blue. "Why don't you rest before supper? I dragged you around more than I should have today."

Jenn just nodded and let him usher her out of the

den, down the hall and to her rooms, where he left her on her own as he headed back outside.

As she stepped into the lush sitting room portion of her suite, she did some firm reprimanding of herself.

She knew that it was a warning sign that her spirits had elevated when she'd learned that that phone call from Matt's Denver friend hadn't offered a quick fix that might have taken her away.

A warning sign she needed to heed.

Even if she was more inclined to follow primal urges instead.

Chapter Seven

After dinner that evening the McDermots and Jenn all went back to their rooms to change before they went ice skating.

Jenn bundled up in two sweaters—a crew neck over a turtleneck—and added two more pairs of socks to the one she'd had on during the day.

She also redid her hair, brushing it out of the braid it had been in while she'd shopped with Matt and upsweeping it to catch at the back of her head in an oversized clip, letting the curly ends spray around her crown like a geyser.

Then she touched up her blush and mascara and left her rooms as if she didn't have a care in the world. Which was actually how she felt, because something about the evening seemed to discontinue the quest for who she was, freeing her to just enjoy herself.

Buzz wasn't going ice skating and Matt's sister Kate had opted for staying home with him and the kids, but when Jenn reached the entryway she found the rest of the McDermots already there, donning warm outerwear.

Matt was among them, and as Jenn joined the group she only had eyes for him.

He'd changed clothes the same way she had, leaving on his tight jeans and cowboy boots, but adding layers on top. Now, rather than the flannel shirt he'd worn earlier, he had a heavy hunter green fisherman's knit rolled neck sweater that accentuated the color of his eyes and framed his freshly shaven face in a way that threw every chiseled angle into relief.

He looked so good to Jenn that her heart skipped a beat and for a moment she wished they weren't going ice skating at all. She wished they were staying at home so she could be alone with him.

But of course that wouldn't be wise, she reminded herself. There was safety in numbers and it was probably a good thing they were going out.

Still though, as he helped her on with the heavy fleece-lined coat, she couldn't deny the longing deep down inside to have him all to herself.

"Coat, gloves, earmuffs, muffler," Matt said, doing a verbal checklist of her cold-weather gear as he gave her the once-over. "Looks like we've got you bundled up enough."

"You, too," she said, looking at him from incredibly handsome head to booted feet as if she were making sure he was dressed warm enough when in fact she was just feasting on the sight of his untamed hair and sexily dimpled chin and big broad shoulders and thick thighs.

"We're all set. How 'bout you guys?" Matt asked the rest of his family.

Everyone agreed they were ready, too, and so they moved outside where a huge old-fashioned sleigh waited for them.

It was made of a whitewashed wood with three rows of bench seats.

The first—the driver's seat—was about a foot higher than the rest, while the other two were sunk within carved side walls that rose and dipped like makeshift ocean waves on a carnival ride.

Two horses were hitched to the front, both in red winter blankets with Christmas bells attached to the hems. Thick clouds of steam wafted from the animals' nostrils on the crisp winter air where the snow had slowed to a few lazy flakes drifting from a still overcast black sky.

Apparently it had been decided at some point that Matt was doing the driving to the lake because the other two couples climbed into the center and rear seats, leaving the front for Jenn and Matt.

Matt seemed to know what he was doing, though. Just as his brothers had done for their wives, he swept up the warm woolen lap robe that lay folded on the seat and tucked it around his legs and Jenn's. Then he took the reins, made a clicking noise and gave a slight slap of the leather straps. The horses set off in a canter, jingling Christmas bells in the winter night.

No one talked over the sound of the bells as the sleigh glided through the snow-covered countryside. But Jenn was very conscious of the man beside her even if he didn't have much to say.

It was crazy, really, because there they both were, separated by layers of clothes, heavy coats, gloves and the lap robe that covered it all, and yet she was extremely aware of the heat coming from his big body—enough to keep the chill of the frigid clime at bay.

She was also aware of his thigh touching hers just slightly and of the sparks that contact ignited all through her. Of the straightness of his spine against the wooden backrest. Of the massiveness of his biceps bulging the suede of his coat. Of the strength in gloved hands that were gentle on the reins at the same time they managed to command the giant beasts who pulled the sleigh.

Out of the corner of her eye she was even aware of every nuance of his profile, of the perfection of his square brow and aquiline nose and perfect masculine lips and that chin...

That chin that she wanted to trace with a finger that could dip into the dimple...

Or maybe trace with the tip of her tongue instead...

That thought caused Jenn to take a quick, involuntary gasp of icy air, and it drew Matt's attention at exactly the moment she didn't want it.

He glanced over at her and said, ''Cold?''

"No," she answered too fast.

But he seemed to have made up his mind that that was the reason for her sharp intake of breath and he reached an arm around her to pull her close to his side. Close enough that now his thigh against hers was nothing slight, it was a firm, massive presence. Close enough that her shoulder was under his arm, her arm running the length of his rib cage. Close enough that she could have melted into the pure warmth and power of him.

"I'm okay. Really," she insisted.

But it didn't change anything. He stayed just the way he was, guiding the horses with the reins in one hand while his other held Jenn close and made her head go light and her blood run quick and hot.

"We'll be there in a minute and there'll be a bon-fire," he assured.

But Jenn only heard it peripherally as every one of her senses seemed to fill itself with him and leave rational thought at a minimum.

And then the bright glow of that promised bonfire shone up ahead. Other sleighs and skimobiles and a few horse-drawn wagons came into view, too, along with the people those conveyances had brought to what Matt had referred to as Make-out Lake.

"What'd I tell you?" he said with a nod in that direction as they drew ever nearer.

Then a softly muttered "Whoa" from Matt brought the horses to a standstill at a spot not far from where the darkness was alight with golden fire-glow and folks were drawn around it, variously warming hands or feet or fannies.

Hellos went out all around as the McDermots climbed from the sleigh.

Matt helped Jenn down and then kept a hand at the small of her back as they joined the crowd.

That hand didn't help tame the wild thoughts that being so near to him had inspired. The same wild thoughts that were also not helped by the sense of them as more than just two people who had been thrown together, a sense of them as a couple.

Skates were being rented from the back of a wagon, and once everyone who needed a pair had one, they sat on the logs to put them on.

Matt needed both his hands to lace his skates so Jenn was finally free of his touch and all it elicited from her.

And even though she knew it was better not to have him touching her, not to have her head muddled all the more by the response she just couldn't stop, she still missed his touch and couldn't help wishing they could forget about ice skating and just stay cuddled up near the fire the way some couples were doing.

But instead, within minutes, they both had on their skates and were headed for the frozen lake.

"It's a little late to ask, but do you think you know how to skate?" Matt said along the way.

"They don't feel foreign on my feet," she answered, even as she recognized the urge to pretend they did, maybe even to stumble on them, just to have the return of his supporting arm around her back.

But she didn't do it. Instead she said, "What

about you? I wouldn't think there would be a lot of ice skating in Texas.''

''I played hockey,'' he answered as she took her first steps out onto the ice.

That was when Jenn discovered she was actually pretty good at skating, keeping her balance and gliding as gracefully as he did into the circular pattern the other skaters were following around the outer perimeter of the lake.

''Looks like hockey paid off for you,'' she said after a few minutes of watching Matt's abilities.

''You're not too bad yourself,'' he returned the compliment.

''What else did you do as a kid? Football? Soccer? Basketball?'' she asked then.

''Do you mean was I a jock?''

''Were you?''

''I think I was more cowboy than anything. But I played a little football, too. Contact sports—living in my house prepared me well for them.''

''Why is that?''

''I'm the youngest brother. You don't live with three older brothers and not get toughened up.''

''Were they mean to you?'' she cooed, teasing him.

He laughed. ''Brutal. I had to earn the right to hang out with them—which, of course, was what I wanted to do from the minute I could walk.''

''And how did you earn the right?''

''Doing just about anything you can think of. The harder and more miserable the better. Eatin' bugs, jumpin' out of haylofts, catchin' greased pigs, ridin' unbroken horses, gettin' strung up by my feet from trees and thrown into ponds before I could swim. And then there were the fights and the wrestlin' matches. We were so cantankerous my poor mother said it was like livin' in an animal cage at the zoo.''

"So you were a bad kid, huh?''

"Just all-boy boys. I didn't get into any kind of trouble with the law or anything. Well, except for doin' some mailbox bashin' in high school that got me caught.''

"How about school? Were you a good student?''

Somehow they'd gotten away from the crowd and were in the center of the lake making a smaller circle of their own. Matt moved out far enough ahead of her to turn around and skate backward as they talked, which gave her a moonlit view of him that started everything inside her churning again just when she'd thought she'd succeeded at calming it all down.

"I was a pretty good student, yeah,'' he answered. "We didn't dare bring home less than Bs or my old man—my father—would give us what-for. He said my mother's family may have thought he was a no-good but his kids were gonna prove it wrong.''

"A no-good?'' Jenn repeated.

"That must have been said somewhere along the way and it stuck. Harsh words get spoken in anger, you know.''

"So you kids paid for a fight between Buzz and your parents that happened even before you were born?''

"That's about it. Not that it didn't serve us all well. Education is important and I'll be tough on my kids, too, if I ever have any."

"Will you ever have any?"

"Someday," he said but he didn't seem to want to get into that so Jenn didn't pursue it.

Instead she said, "Which of your brothers were you closest to growing up?"

"Bax. That twin thing between Ry and Shane is hard to penetrate. They've always been each other's best friend, so that left Bax and me teaming up once I'd won my place with them all. But Kate and I are pretty close, too. Probably because we're only a year apart in age."

Jenn nodded and lost herself in thought for a moment before Matt said, "Wonderin' if you have any brothers or sisters out there somewhere?"

Jenn laughed. "Yes, as a matter of fact I was. And thinking that it doesn't feel like I do. But maybe that just comes from not being able to remember them."

"Maybe. But I think brothers and sisters—family—leave a stamp on you. Seems like you'd have a sense of important people in your life even if you can't remember them specifically."

"Maybe," she allowed.

Matt spun on his skates then and ended up beside her once more, this time linking his elbow through hers. "What would you say to some hot chocolate or cider and a few minutes by the fire?"

"I'd say oh good because my knees are freezing."

He laughed at that, a deep chuckle that sounded as if it came from inside a barrel, and guided them both back to the lake's edge.

It was a tactical error, though, Jenn realized as they joined the people sipping hot beverages around the bonfire. Because by then word had apparently spread about her to anyone who hadn't known before and, like that afternoon, folks began to come up to be introduced and to have her do her trick of telling them what she knew about them.

They were all nice people, but that didn't change the fact that it ended her time alone with Matt. Time Jenn had been enjoying so much, she most certainly hadn't wanted it to end.

But once things got started in that direction, that was where they continued, on the ice and off, until the cold finally got to enough of the McDermots that they all decided to call it a night.

It helped salvage the evening, though, when Ry took up the reins for the drive home and Matt and Jenn got the rear seat in the sleigh.

By then, huddling together for warmth really did seem like a necessity and that was how they ended up, sitting close together with the lap robe tightly tucked in around them both, and Matt's arm once again wrapping Jenn's shoulder to keep her nestled against his side.

It was so cozy she hardly noticed the chill that had finally inched its way through all the layers of clothes and could no longer be chased away. She was more aware of Matt again and how good it felt to be snuggled up with him.

"Is my nose as red as yours is?" he asked when they were on their way.

She looked closely, only too happy for the excuse to take in the sight of that gloriously handsome face. "Pretty red," she told him because it was true.

He leaned over enough to rub hers with his, as if that would make some difference.

"Why do you suppose they say Eskimos kiss that way?" he asked in a voice that was suddenly deeper, richer, more intimate.

"I can't imagine," she answered, her own voice quiet and more dreamy-sounding than she'd intended.

"Doesn't seem likely to me. Not when the real thing is so much better."

He was looking into her eyes with those penetrating green ones of his, holding them as surely as he was holding her. And again she started to think about him kissing her, just the way she'd thought about it the night before.

But no sooner had the thought occurred to her than she pushed it away, because she didn't want to be as disappointed as she'd been then.

So when he actually did kiss her, it caught her by surprise.

All of a sudden there he was, his agile lips pressed to hers, slightly parted and somehow warm even though his nose was like an icicle where it barely brushed her cheek.

And there she was, too, kissing him back, answering with parted lips of her own that savored what she'd been thinking about so much in the last twenty-four hours.

But all too soon the kiss was over, almost before it had begun—or at least that was how it seemed to Jenn.

Matt ended it and looked into her eyes once more.

"Guess I probably shouldn't have done that," he said softly.

Jenn wanted to ask why not but she didn't. She didn't really have to. She knew why he thought he shouldn't have kissed her. It was because no matter how much it might seem like they were just two people who had met and found themselves attracted to each other, that wasn't what they were. They were two people caught up by fate in circumstances that couldn't have been more bizarre. Circumstances in which neither of them knew who she was or where she'd come from or what she'd left behind.

And attraction or no attraction, they were circumstances that screamed for caution. For self-control.

Neither of them said anything else the remainder of the ride home. And Matt didn't kiss her again.

But he also didn't pull away.

Instead they stayed cuddled beneath the lap robe, his arm around her shoulders, her thigh pressed to the length of his, their breaths silent clouds that mingled and mixed on the night air.

Jenn was convinced it wasn't just for warmth that he kept her close beside him, but also because no matter how much they both knew they should be fighting what was happening between them, at that moment neither of them could break the connection that felt so good.

When they reached the ranch once more, Jenn wondered if he would kiss her good-night when they got to her bedroom door.

But he didn't.

She thought he wanted to. Or maybe it was her own desires she was projecting onto him when he lingered there in the hallway. But he didn't.

He only explained that they were all taking the sleigh out again the next day to cut down their Christmas tree and then told her to sleep well before he turned to his own rooms.

But even once she was alone, slipping into her bed for the night, that single kiss seemed to linger on her lips like a whisper.

She couldn't help touching her fingertips to them, to that same spot where Matt's mouth had been. She couldn't help remembering just how much she'd liked his kiss.

But worse than that, she couldn't help wishing there had been many, many more of them.

Chapter Eight

Jenn was wide-awake early the next morning, jolted from sleep by another dream. Another dream of herself as that old woman she'd dreamed of before.

Not that it was the same dream. The first dream had been innocuous. Not unpleasant. But this one…

In this one she hadn't started out as the old woman. This time, when the dream had begun, she'd looked like herself.

She'd been at the McDermots' ranch again, but it had been exactly the way it was now.

She and Matt had been together. And of course he'd been as traffic-stoppingly handsome and charming and sweet as he really was.

He'd kissed her in the dream. Just the way he'd kissed her the night before. But in the dream, the moment his lips had met hers, she'd turned into the old woman and he'd ended the kiss immediately.

She'd assumed it was because she'd changed into the old woman. That she'd repulsed him. But then she'd realized she was hiding the shaving kit filled with money behind her back and that was what had turned him off. He'd known it wasn't hers. He'd known it was bad money. He knew she was bad for having it.

And he hadn't wanted anything to do with her because of it.

That was when she'd come awake with an adrenaline rush as severe as if she were being chased.

She didn't understand it but the dream had made her feel as awful as any hideous nightmare might have. Scared and embarrassed and ashamed. And although it was irrational, she couldn't shake the sense that it was some kind of premonition. Of Matt being repulsed by her when he found out she had that money.

No amount of telling herself it was only a dream, that it didn't mean anything, that probably the money had come from something perfectly innocent and honest helped to make the ominous feeling go away.

She got out of bed and went into the bathroom to shower and begin the day, hoping that would help her escape the lingering effects of the dream.

And it *was* only a dream, she kept telling herself again and again, as she let the steamy water run over her face and hair. Just a dream that didn't mean anything.

Except that it had renewed her negative feelings about that money and canceled any idea she might have had about confiding in Matt that it existed.

But what was the point of thinking about that money? Regardless of how hard she tried, she couldn't recall anything about it and the more she worried, the tighter seemed her mind's lock on her memory. So didn't that make it harmful?

She thought it did.

Then stop, she told herself firmly. Think about the weather. Or going to cut down the Christmas tree. Or breakfast. Or what to wear…

But thoughts of the dream and the money stubbornly persisted.

The only thought able to replace them were memories of the real kiss she and Matt had shared the night before.

Ah, the kiss…

She'd liked that kiss. There were no two ways about it. And just replaying it in her mind transported her from the ugly feelings of the dream.

But then, who *wouldn't* have liked that kiss?

Matt was definitely good at it. His mouth against hers had been soft, slightly commanding, enticing, intriguing, inviting. He'd applied just the right amount of pressure, of insistence. Just the right amount of everything.

She'd wanted the kiss to go on and on. To evolve into two kisses. And three. She'd wanted to have his arms wrap her more tightly than they had. To have him pull her so close that her breasts would have been flattened against that broad expanse of rock-solid chest.

She'd wanted to feel his big hands splayed out on her back. Or exploring more than her back.

She'd wanted to be swept up onto his lap. To feel proof that the same things that had been coming alive in her were coming alive in him...

Oh, dear.

Jenn opened her eyes, unaware of when she'd closed them, of when what had started out as simple thoughts about that kiss had wandered into much more treacherous territory.

Territory she had no business venturing into.

Boundaries, she reminded herself. Stay within the boundaries.

Of course, that kiss of the previous evening had been outside those boundaries to begin with. What did she expect thinking about it to be?

But boundaries or no boundaries, that kiss definitely hadn't felt as if she were doing anything wrong.

It had felt wonderful.

But that was part of the problem, she realized.

It had felt so wonderful—so much more wonderful than she'd even imagined it might feel—that now it was all the more difficult to remain within those boundaries. Now all she wanted to do was say to heck with any boundaries. She wanted to crash through them and right into Matt's arms.

But she couldn't do that. She had to maintain some limits. She really did.

Which meant no more kissing.

And no more being carried away by an imagination that only began at the innocent kiss and took things so much farther than that.

Jenn had finished her shower by then and she stepped out of the stall to dry herself off with the same intensity she'd used to wash. An intensity born of racing thoughts and the mounting excitement that went with them.

Maybe thinking about the dream was better, she decided.

Remembering how bad she'd felt in the dream would allow her to keep some control over what was happening between her and Matt. Some control over her thoughts. Over her emotions.

Because maybe the dream was telling her something after all. Maybe it was warning her that when she found out who she was and why she was in Elk Creek and what that money was all about, Matt was going to be repulsed by her.

And that would be so much worse if she let things go too far beforehand.

So maybe she should take that warning to heart.

But as she slipped into her bathrobe she was very much afraid that more than taking the warning to heart, she was taking Matt to heart. Every minute she was with him only seemed to compound her feelings for him.

And she *did* have feelings for him. Much as she wished she didn't and tried to extinguish them.

But how could she extinguish something that seemed to have a life of its own? Like trick birthday candles that kept re-igniting even after someone had worked like crazy to blow them out.

All it took was one glimpse of his face, one smile tossed her way, one note of his voice, one whiff of his aftershave, and there she was, putty in his hands.

Then something else occurred to her, something even more disturbing than the fact that she was having no luck resisting his allure.

What if, deep down, she didn't want to remember anything because when she regained her memory she'd have no more reason to stay with him?

No, surely that couldn't be why her memory was so elusive.

Could it?

She sincerely hoped not. That really would be crazy, and unfair to Matt. Rescuing her didn't mean he'd signed on for the long haul, after all.

But on the off chance that her attraction to him was impeding her mental progress, she really did need to resist it, she told herself.

No matter what her feelings for him were, no matter how attracted to him she was, she had to contain it and that was all there was to it. She had to contain it at least until she knew who she was and that she was completely free and worthy of a man like him.

Until that time, she just wouldn't let anything else happen between them.

No matter how difficult that might be.

She owed him that.

But what if her memory came back? she proposed

to herself. What if it came back and she knew she was completely free and worthy of a man like him?

Now *that* would be a horse of a different color.

Suddenly she felt a whole new motivation to have her amnesia resolved or to find out something concrete about herself.

Because regardless of how determined she was not to let anything else happen between them, she wasn't honestly sure she could accomplish it. She wasn't honestly sure if even the best intentions were powerful enough to really extinguish those trick birthday candles.

"So come back soon, memory," she whispered to herself. "And let me know this is all okay."

In the meantime she'd just have to hope she could hold out....

Once again the sleigh was the mode of transportation as the McDermots and Jenn headed out to cut down a Christmas tree at one o'clock that afternoon. Only this time Kate McDermot, little Andrew and Evie Lee were also onboard.

Matt took the reins again and he and Jenn shared the front bench with both kids, Evie Lee sitting between them and Andrew on Matt's lap.

Matt was good with them, Jenn realized as she watched him fueling their excitement with talk of Santa Claus and letting them each hold the reins to get a feel for them. And not only was he good with the kids, he genuinely seemed to be enjoying them.

He *should* have children of his own someday, she

thought, recalling his comment the night before about wanting them. He'd be a great dad.

She just didn't want to think of his being a great dad to any kids who weren't also hers.

And even though that was an unrealistic, premature and inappropriate thought to begin with, today it seemed even more far-fetched because, unless she was mistaken, he was keeping his distance from her.

Not that he wasn't every bit as attentive and friendly and nice. There was just something slightly remote about him since they'd met up in the kitchen for breakfast. After breakfast he'd gone to do chores in the barn, leaving her on her own with his sisters-in-law and Kate until lunchtime. And at lunchtime he hadn't made a point of sitting beside her in the breakfast nook the way he'd done for every other meal they'd had there.

It was the kiss that had made the difference. Jenn was sure of it. Hadn't he said he shouldn't have done it? Obviously he'd meant it. So now he was rectifying the situation that had developed between them.

And although intellectually Jenn knew without a doubt that that was exactly the right thing to do, she still suffered deep, deep pangs of disappointment that he wasn't crossing those boundaries she'd talked herself into believing they needed to abide by.

It helped a little that she didn't think it was easy for him to keep that distance, though. Because more than once she'd caught him watching her when he didn't think she was looking. Studying her with eyes

that almost seemed hungry. And when they'd all begun to climb into the sleigh, he'd reached for her
waist with both hands to help her up and then
snapped them back and barely taken her elbow instead, as if a force of willpower at the last moment
had kept him in line.

So maybe, she told herself, if they were both of
a like mind when it came to cooling things off between them, they'd have more success at it.

Which should have been encouraging.

But for some reason, as he drove the sleigh across
snow-covered fields and the sound of his voice joking with his niece and nephew was all around her,
it felt just the opposite.

The tree the McDermots had picked out ahead of
time was a perfect pine about a mile from the house.

To Jenn's knowledge, she'd never cut down her
own Christmas tree because the whole process
seemed new and unusual rather than the tiniest bit
familiar.

It was the men who did most of the work.

Since Matt was said to be the best with a rope,
that became his job.

He laid out three lines behind the tree and lassoed
the top with three more, handing the ends—one
each—to Tallie, Maya and Kate after he'd positioned them in a semicircle around one side of the
evergreen.

"Keep the ropes taut and pull on them the whole
time. They're long so you should be plenty far

enough away from the tree when it falls but still make sure you back up,'' he instructed.

Then, while Jenn kept the kids out of the way, the men took turns with a broadax.

Matt had explained when he'd loaded the ax on the sleigh that they could have used a chain saw but it was the McDermot tradition to do it the old-fashioned way, putting muscle into it.

Apparently the tradition also involved some fierce competition between the brothers who good-naturedly heckled whoever was wielding the ax at any given time.

But it was a sight to behold for Jenn.

At least it was when it was Matt's turn.

He opted for taking off the heavy suede coat he had on again, freeing long arms he made quite a show of stretching and shaking out while his brothers goaded him about wasting time.

Then, in his flannel shirtsleeves, tight jeans, cowboy boots and leather gloves, he finally took the ax in hand. Pretending it was a baseball bat, he took a few practice swings before he actually got down to business and approached the tree for the final whacks that would fell it.

Jenn watched him put that strong back behind every swing, stretching the flannel tight across his shoulders as his thick thighs braced for each blow and absorbed the shock when ax met wood.

It didn't help all of her resolutions to be standing behind him, either, because that also put his derriere in view. And try as she might, she couldn't keep her eyes from wandering where they shouldn't have wandered.

It was just such a terrific rear end. Perfect, in fact. Teasing her from behind twin pockets that cupped it like a lover's palm...

His derriere was where she was looking when he suddenly stepped away from the tree and yelled an exuberant, "Here she goes!"

Apparently that was his brothers' cue to shout for their wives and sister to "Pull! Pull!"

Excitement mounted as the crack and splinter of the trunk echoed through the cold countryside, and for a moment the big fir seemed to hover in midair as if it might not fall after all.

But then gravity got the best of it and it lumbered in a graceful arc to the ground amidst cheers and hoots and hollers and clapping and children jumping up and down.

The men got busy again as soon as the tree hit the ground.

The three ropes Matt had laid out in the snow were exactly where the tree had landed and those were pulled tight to tie the branches and fashion the tree into a compact arrow. Then the men dragged it to the rear of the sleigh where they hoisted it across the runners that jutted out behind the back seat, tying it on so they didn't lose it on the way home.

And that was that for cutting down a Christmas tree.

Everyone piled into the sleigh again where Kate poured cups of hot chocolate from a thermos so they could have a warm treat before the horses were set into motion once more, this time by Shane.

Matt and Jenn occupied the rear seat they'd shared the night before for the return trip. Alone again beneath their lap robe.

"So how was that?" Matt asked when they were settled in.

She knew what he meant. He was asking if she'd enjoyed watching the tree cutting. And it was on the tip of Jenn's tongue to say it was magnificent. Or that *he* was.

But she joked instead. "Fishing for compliments?"

"You bet," he said with a big grin.

"Okay. Good boy," she praised as if he were a dog she'd been training, teasing him still.

Matt caught on. "You gonna toss me a bone?"

"Sorry, I'm fresh out."

His grin turned rakish. "You could rub my belly. We dogs love that," he said in a tone full of lasciviousness.

"Maybe later," she answered with a laugh.

"Is that a promise?"

She laughed again. "No, it isn't."

"Damn," he muttered with a sigh that made a cloud on the air, grinning still.

But something in that silly exchange—or maybe in the tree cutting before it—seemed to have weakened that willpower Jenn thought had kept him at a distance earlier in the day because he stretched his arm around her shoulders then, pulling her closer beside him as if that was where she just naturally belonged.

"Guess I better take my reward where I can get it," he said, as if having his arm around her qualified as that reward.

And that was how they stayed for the remainder of the ride back to the ranch—snuggled together beneath the lap robe just as they'd been the night before, when he'd kissed her.

So much for distance and boundaries and will-power and resolves, Jenn thought.

But somehow she just couldn't find the resources to make herself move away.

What was left of the afternoon once they got back home was spent with the men making a stand for the tree and the women carrying boxes of decorations from a storage room into the big living room with its matching leather sofas positioned around the fireplace.

It was time for dinner once those jobs were done and after a joint-effort meal of steaks, baked potatoes, green beans, salad and bread, everyone finally got down to trimming the tree under Buzz's watchful eye.

Jenn appreciated being included as if she were a part of the family, and as she helped to string lights, hang bulbs and ornaments, and toss strands of tinsel, she began to have vague flashbacks of other Christmases.

They weren't clear enough to reveal anything useful to her. She just had a sense that those other

Christmases were far more quiet than the boisterous joking and singing and laughter of the large Mc-Dermot clan.

Had she spent those other Christmases alone? she wondered, feeling sad to think that she might have.

But this wasn't the time or place for that sadness and she decided that whatever was or wasn't in her past, she should enjoy this moment now, while she could.

And because of that she pushed away the lonely sense of other Christmases and threw herself whole-heartedly into the decorations.

In fact, she was still going strong at eleven when the tree had been completed and all the figurines, candles and other mementos had been set out to adorn the house. By then the kids had fallen asleep on the couches, though, and the adults were ready to call it a night, too.

It was Matt's suggestion that everyone else go on to bed, that he'd clean up, and Jenn was only too happy to volunteer her services as well.

She told herself she was just being a good house-guest. That she owed Matt some assistance after all he'd done for her. That since she wasn't tired she might as well pitch in.

But she knew that even though that was all true, it wasn't the real reason.

The real reason was that she couldn't pass up the opportunity to have him to herself—something she hadn't had all day.

So the rest of the McDermots scattered to the bed-rooms and Jenn got the wish that was in direct conflict with what her goal should have been: She ended up alone with Matt.

Cleanup was mainly a matter of hauling boxes back into storage, and as they did that, it crossed Jenn's mind that as soon as they were finished Matt might just say good-night, too, and go off to his own room. Especially since the brief closeness they'd shared in the sleigh on the way home hadn't continued once they'd gotten back. Matt had again turned as remote as he'd been earlier in the day.

But once the house was in order he didn't just say good-night and disappear. Instead, as they stacked the last of the empty boxes, he said, "I always agree to do the straightening up so I can sit and enjoy the finished product with everyone else out of the way. What do you say to a little mulled cider in front of the Christmas tree?"

"I'd say it sounds nice," Jenn answered, knowing that even that much was crossing her imaginary boundary again but unable to deny herself what she wanted more than she'd admitted until that moment.

Matt gave orders for her to turn off everything but the tree lights and those that shone through the windows of the Victorian houses and shops in the porcelain village that lined the mantel, and he went for the cider.

By the time he returned with two steaming mugs, Jenn was sitting on the sofa that faced the tree. She'd purposely chosen to hug one end of the sofa rather than to sit in the center of it so that if Matt still wanted to maintain his distance he could opt for the other end.

But he didn't choose the other end. Instead he handed her a mug and sat right beside her, propping his booted feet on the coffee table, crossing his ankles and wiggling around until he was comfortable. He was so close to her that his thigh ran the length of hers, pressed seamlessly together to the knee.

"She's a beauty, don't you think?" he said after a sigh that let her know he was winding down for the evening.

Jenn forced her eyes away from him to take a good long look at the tree, at the results of all their labors.

The beamed ceiling of the living room was at least twelve feet high and the star that crowned the top of the Christmas tree was nestled between two of those beams, brushing the ceiling itself. From there the tree's branches opened to a full eight feet radius on bottom.

There was no unifying theme to the tree's decorations but it was full of ornaments that all seemed to have come with a story of their own. There were those memorializing births and anniversaries. Those made lovingly by hand, some from generations before. Those that were just plain fun, and others that were a bit odd-looking, like the panda bear fashioned with a painted walnut shell body, a hazelnut head and tiny pom-pom arms, feet and ears. But all of them reflected one or another of the McDermots' taste and not a single ornament lacked a special meaning to someone.

Woven among them were strings of tiny white and large multicolored lights. It was an interesting effect, Jenn thought, like big bright jewels amidst the pure glow of the crystals. All in all, it made for a homey, traditional tree that she had to agree qualified as a beauty.

"Any of our Christmas activities today spur a memory?" Matt asked after they'd each sipped their cider.

"No," Jenn said, not wanting to bring that feeling of loneliness and sadness she'd had into this moment with Matt. Especially when it hadn't been productive or served any purpose.

"I wish something had spurred my memory," she added. "It would be nice to know a few facts."

"Mmm" was all he said to concede the point.

Then Jenn changed the subject for no other reason than that the image had come to mind of him with his niece and nephew in the sleigh and again as they'd decorated the tree: Matt holding them up to put ornaments on the high branches and carrying Andrew around on his shoulders so they could work as a team when the little boy got underfoot.

"You're really crazy about Andrew and Evie Lee, aren't you?"

"Christmas is a time for kids."

"Oh, I don't know, I think you'd like having them around anytime."

He smiled sheepishly. "They're fun," he admitted.

"So how come you don't have any of your own yet?" she asked, wondering if he'd avoid discussing it the way he'd seemed to the night before.

But instead he joked. "Last time I checked, it took two to pull off having kids."

"A husband and a wife," she confirmed. "So why don't you have one?"

"A husband?" he asked in mock outrage, purposely misunderstanding her.

"A wife. To have kids with. Or is there someone already in line for the job and I just haven't met her?"

That last thought had only occurred to her a split second before she'd said it. But once she had, it struck her that it might actually be true. And knowing whether or not it was was suddenly very important to her. She began to wonder if involvement with someone else was why he was reticent to start anything up with her.

The idea didn't make Jenn happy.

In fact, it threatened to ruin the good mood she'd been trying to maintain all evening.

But then Matt gave a nonchalant shrug of his shoulders and said, "No, there's nobody in line for the job of my wife. I just came out of what I *thought* was a serious relationship. A relationship I *thought* was going somewhere permanent."

"But you were wrong?"

"Oh, yeah," he said, drawing the words out ominously.

"You were wrong about things going somewhere permanent?"

"About that and about the woman herself."

"Sounds bad," Jenn observed, interpreting his tone and hoping to prompt him to tell her more by adding, "How were you wrong about the woman herself?"

He was still staring at the tree even though Jenn had altered her line of vision to look at him. She didn't mind. The sight of his chiseled profile lit by fireglow and the glimmer of the Christmas lights was something she preferred even over the beauty of the tree. And since he didn't seem to notice her staring, she felt free to go on feasting on the sight of him.

But he waited so long to answer her question, and from the frown that pulled his brows nearly together, she began to wonder if she'd ventured into forbidden territory.

Then, after another drink of his cider, he finally said, "Sarah—that was her name—was a very secretive person. At first that was her allure. I was intrigued by what she didn't say about herself. And of course I figured her secrets were all probably just small things."

"But they weren't."

"Not by a long shot. She'd come to stay with a cousin who'd moved into the town nearest my family's ranch in Texas—that was how I met her. I didn't know her cousin very well, didn't know anything about Sarah, but she was great looking and liked to have a good time, and her cousin was a decent enough woman so why should I have thought Sarah was anything but a decent woman, too? Plus, that air of secrecy went pretty far in stringing me along. I was hell-bent on solving the mystery. And in the meantime I really fell for her."

He said that as if he'd received a death sentence and Jenn just waited patiently for him to go on because she could see this wasn't easy for him to tell.

"Then I found out what she was keeping secret."

"Something pretty bad," Jenn guessed.

"Well, she wasn't a serial killer," he said. "But come to find out, Sarah had deserted her family. She'd abandoned two small kids in a gas station with a note instructing that they be returned to their father. She'd also cleared out the family's bank account and was staying with her cousin to lie low so her husband wouldn't find her."

"Oh," Jenn said because she didn't know what else *to* say. And she wasn't too sure she *didn't* consider a mother abandoning her children in a gas station almost as bad as a serial killer.

Matt continued, so intent on what he was telling her that he didn't seem to notice that she hadn't commented further. "It came as a big surprise to me when her cousin finally took me aside and told me what was going on. Sarah had her thinkin' we were just friends, that there wasn't anything romantic between us. But when the cousin heard through the grapevine that I'd been looking at engagement rings, she thought I should be warned."

"I'd say that qualifies as a surprise, all right."

"And definitely not the kind I ever want to have again."

It was a simple statement on the surface. But underlying it was so much more that Jenn heard in his voice.

Like the fact that she was another mystery woman

to him. A mystery woman who could be running from something just the way his Sarah had been. So Matt was leery.

And he had every right to be, Jenn acknowledged. Especially when she recalled that money in the shaving kit and how bad it still made her feel. Money she was keeping a secret from him.

"I'm sorry," she said, not only expressing her sympathy but also apologizing in part for what might be her own similarities to Sarah. Although of course Matt couldn't know that.

He shrugged, turning his handsome head and apparently focusing on her again, looking as if he were letting go of the pall that had come with the subject of his past. "It's okay. I got out before it was too late."

"But not before you had feelings for her," Jenn guessed.

He smiled a small, wry smile. "Yeah," he conceded.

"So you were hurt."

Matt's smile broadened into a grin and he leaned slightly toward her as if to confide in her. "Men don't admit to gettin' hurt. We say we've been burned or blindsided or gut-punched or somethin' more macho."

Jenn laughed, grateful that he'd lightened the tone again. "Oh, excuse me," she joked.

But then she felt inclined to fish a little more, maybe hoping he'd refute what she was thinking. "So are you hearing shrieking alarms telling you to keep away from me since even *I* don't know who I am? I mean… Well, probably not, because it isn't as if we're… Well, probably not. Never mind," she amended as she realized belatedly that the initial comment sounded presumptuous and he wouldn't be hearing alarms over just some woman he'd done a good deed for.

He took her off the hook, though. "I'm hearin' a few alarms," he admitted.

He rolled onto his hip then, bracing on the arm he stretched along the sofa back behind her so that he was suddenly much, much closer than he had been, looking down at her, studying her face. "The trouble is, I'm not doin' too well at listenin' to 'em."

"No?" she asked, not intending for it to come out in the breathy whisper it had.

But it was the effect of those dark green eyes that seemed to penetrate hers. And he was near enough for her to smell the lingering trace of his aftershave and the scent of the mulling spices on his breath. To see the masculine texture of his skin and the way the dimple dipped into his chin.

And she liked it all so much.

She liked *him* so much.

"No," he repeated, "I'm definitely not doin' too well listenin' to those alarms. Even though I know you really are a mystery woman and aren't just puttin' it on the way Sarah was, you have me worried some. That's somethin' I have to 'fess up to," he said in a voice that was low and quiet and just a little husky. "But there's other stuff goin' on that always seems to push that worry aside and take me over.''

''I know the feeling,'' she said, more to herself than to him.

''Feelings—there's that word again. And they're the problem. I'm havin' feelings I know I shouldn't be havin'.''

But apparently his feelings were as powerful as those Jenn was in constant battle with because even talking about them didn't stop him from reaching across her to set first his mug and then hers on the end table next to the couch.

Then he settled back the way he'd been before, only this time his hand came to rest along the side of her jaw to raise her face higher.

''How about you? Hearin' any shrieking alarms of your own?'' he asked.

''Shrieking,'' she confirmed.

''What're you doin' about 'em?''

She smiled and laughed just a bit. ''Ignoring them most of the time.''

He laughed, too. And then he sobered mere moments before he slowly lowered his mouth to hers in a kiss that was soft and sweet.

A kiss that changed and changed again so that that one single kiss seemed like more as it went to deeper and deeper levels. His lips parted over hers, urging hers to part, too, with a tongue that traced the bare inside of them and coaxed them to relax. A warm, gentle tongue that gave notice it was coming for a visit, meeting hers tip to tip in a circle dance.

Somewhere in Jenn's mind there was the echo of that alarm they'd talked about, warning her that she shouldn't be doing this. But she just couldn't listen to it. She was too lost in the feel of that adept mouth open wide over hers now, of the waltz of that talented tongue leading her step by step, of his hand toying with her hair in back and his other hand caressing her face. Of her own hand at the nape of his thick, corded neck where even the bristle of his hairline felt masculine and sexy and wonderful.

She was too lost in the weight of one thigh that had somehow come across her legs where they were stretched to the coffee table along with his. Too lost in the warm velvet miracle of his mouth as their kiss went on and on and taught her how just kissing like that could awaken every sense, every need, every desire to flow through her veins like warm honey.

She might not have known much about herself but at that moment she knew she was right where she wanted to be. She knew that there was something about Matt that fed her soul, her spirit, and made everything else unimportant. Completely unimportant.

But just when thoughts of things they could do along with that incredible kiss began to play at the corners of her mind, Matt put everything into rewind. His tongue bid hers goodbye. His lips lingered over hers for only a moment before leaving them, returning for one—no, two more—soft, chaste kisses before he stopped completely.

Then he sighed again, closed his eyes and dropped his forehead to the top of her head. "See?

What'd I tell you? I'm not doin' well at all listenin' to those alarms.''

"Me, either," she said while she fought not to rekindle that kiss herself and maybe start up even more that she knew would really be crossing the line.

They stayed that way for a while, neither of them moving so as not to break what was left of their connection. And again Jenn knew that being so close to him, his hand massaging the back of her neck, his head pressed to hers, the warmth of his big body seeping into her pores, only made the ultimate ending of this more difficult.

So when she finally could, she said, "It's been a long day." In truth it didn't seem as if it had been long enough if it ended before he carried her off to his bed and made love to her.

"Yeah," he agreed on the gust of yet another sigh, rolling and straightening away from her at once and getting to his feet.

Then he held out a hand for her to take and said, "Come on. I'll walk you to your room and we'll lock ourselves behind two separate doors for safe keepin'."

That didn't have anywhere near the appeal of what had gone through her mind just before he'd said it. But it was what they had to do and Jenn knew it.

So she took his hand—because she couldn't refuse herself at least that—slipping into the strong, callused palm as if it were something she'd been doing forever, and stood, too.

Together they turned off the Christmas lights, closed the glass door on the fireplace and headed for their rooms.

Matt kissed her again when they got there, but it was such a simple little buss it was anticlimactic after what they'd just indulged in on the couch. And then he opened her bedroom door and pointed inside as if ordering her into a cell.

Or maybe that was just how it seemed to Jenn, as if leaving him was a punishment of exile.

She went, though, hearing him close the door behind her even before she'd turned to say good-night.

But she didn't hear him go the rest of the way to his own room right away. Instead she could tell he was still outside her door and he stayed there for so long she wondered if he was ever going to go or if he might open her door again and come in after all.

Then she finally heard him move those few feet down the hallway to his own rooms, closing that door securely, too.

But still it wasn't easy for her to accept that that was all she was going to have of him when her whole body, her whole being, was craving so much more.

And when she forced herself to get undressed and into bed for the night it was with thoughts of how nearby Matt was—just in the next room—and how little it would take for them to be together.

If only so many other things didn't stand in the way...

Chapter Nine

The sky was still a canopy of gray clouds, and big fluffy flakes of snow fell from them for the fifth day in a row. None of the snowfall since the first twenty-four hours had been heavy but it all added up, and Jenn was beginning to think she might not be able to retrieve her car until spring.

Not that she was complaining. There was certainly nothing to complain about in staying at the McDermot ranch, being treated like a member of the family and getting to be with Matt.

But it almost seemed as if Elk Creek were socked in much the way her memory was and that maybe if the clouds in the sky would lift, so might the clouds in her head.

In the meantime, though, what was on the agenda

for that next afternoon was gift-wrapping. She'd volunteered to help Evie Lee since she was the only one in the household who didn't have gifts of her own to wrap.

The nice part of it was that she and Evie Lee got to share the den with Matt while he performed that chore for himself.

Unlike everything else he did, though, he wasn't very coordinated with paper and ribbon, so Jenn ended up helping him as much as she helped Evie Lee. But she didn't mind because he was so jovial and full of Christmas spirit that he made even his ineptitude fun.

"Ho, ho, ho!" he boomed with the completion of each job, making Evie Lee laugh every time she heard it.

"Uncle Matt's silly," the little girl joyfully informed Jenn about the sixth time it happened. "He thinks he's Santa Claus and he's not."

"I am so," he claimed from across the big desk that had been cleared for them all to use as a wrapping table. "Evie Lee Lewis just thinks she knows everything and she doesn't," he countered, teasing his niece.

"Do, too," she answered.

"You? Like what do you know?"

"Lots of stuff. I know Santa Claus lives at the North Pole and him and the elves makes lots of toys all year but he can't make everything so the toy stores help him out and so do the mommies and the daddies sometimes, and so do the other pretend Santas you can talk to in the stores and who rings bells outside of places.''

''That's a lot to know, all right,'' Matt conceded.

But it seemed he'd turned on a faucet of information and Evie Lee kept going.

''I know Santa gots lots of reindeers and every night he goes out to the barn and reads 'em a bedtime story and sometimes he sleeps with 'em, too. And Santa and some of the special elves teaches 'em how to fly by sprinkling 'em with magic flying dust that makes 'em sneeze and wears off in between the times they flies or else they'd be flyin' all the time like birds.''

''Uh-huh,'' Matt said, catching Jenn's eyes with his and grinning as if they were sharing a private joke. She knew that in actuality he was delighting in his niece's storytelling.

But then so was Jenn. She was delighting in the little girl's yarns and in being there with Matt, who she kept snatching glimpses of whenever she got the chance. Even dressed in a faded chambray shirt and a pair of jeans that had seen better days, he still looked eye-poppingly handsome to her.

Evie Lee wasn't finished proving she was a wealth of information, though, and went on.

''I know that Mrs. Santa Claus won't make Santa cookies because she thinks he's too fat and his chlo-lester-lol is prob'ly too high so that's why we leave 'im cookies and milk on Christmas Eve—for a treat he doesn't get the rest of the year.''

''His chlo-lester-lol is high?'' Matt repeated as if

it were the news of the day and neither of them had mispronounced the word.

"Yes. It's some kind of bad stuff my daddy tells people to watch out for," Evie Lee explained.

"I know I hate that chlo-lester-lol stuff," Matt said to Jenn with a grin that warmed her from the top of her head to the tip of her toes.

"Me, too," she agreed.

"And what else do I know?" Evie Lee asked herself, musing so intently that her lips were pursed.

"I know my address and my phone number now, too," she concluded in a train of thought only a six-year-old could follow.

"Okay," Matt said. "What are your address and phone number?"

Evie Lee recited them with a slight singsong in her voice that apparently helped her remember.

"Good girl!" Matt praised when she'd finished.

But Jenn didn't join in this time because something about Evie Lee's recitation of her phone number caused Jenn a mental blip, and a totally different phone number popped into her mind.

A phone number that was just there, without her knowing why or whom it might belong to or what it might mean.

Was it her own?

Maybe it was the number she'd received when the one that had been listed for the address on her driver's license had been put out of service. Certainly it was as clear as a bell ringing in her head, which made it seem like her own number. But without any explanation or qualification, how could she know for sure?

She couldn't, unless she dialed it and found out.

She opened her mouth to tell Matt what had just happened, to enlist him in the call, too, but before the words came out it struck her suddenly that maybe she shouldn't do that.

She wasn't exactly clear on *why* she felt that way, but she did.

Maybe it was because she didn't know what the number might be leading to. Or whom. Or what it might uncover.

For instance, what if it was a man's number? A boyfriend's?

Or what if it led her to some unsavory revelation about herself?

Of course it might lead to nothing at all. It might just be another of those dead ends they'd run into up to now.

But somehow she didn't believe that.

Somehow she knew this phone number was going to open a door.

The problem was, she didn't know what was going to be behind that door. No one seemed to be looking for her and if there was a person on the other end of that phone number who didn't care that she was missing, was it a person she wanted to contact?

Or maybe the phone would ring into an empty apartment where she lived alone.

Or maybe it was her work number and by just

dialing it she would find out who she was and where she was from and everything would fall into place.

So just tell Matt and dial it, she told herself.

But still she couldn't bring herself to let him know about that phone number.

Thinking about it—repeating it in her mind so she didn't forget it—didn't give her the same kind of negative feelings that the money in the shaving kit did. Or that the second dream of herself as an old woman did. Which might be a good sign.

But the number also didn't give her any kind of positive feelings, either.

It was just there, niggling at her to dial it.

Without letting Matt know...

He turned his back just then and she used that moment to write the phone number on a scrap of wrapping paper and slip it into the pocket of the jeans she wore, hating herself for the secrecy he didn't deserve.

But she rationalized it by telling herself it was better for her to call the number and find out what was at the other end of it so she could process the information herself first and then break it to Matt tactfully.

"Jenn?"

The tone of Matt's voice drew her out of her reverie and made her realize he must have said something to her that he was waiting for a response to. A response that was never coming because she'd been so lost in her thoughts that she hadn't heard or been aware of anything going on around her.

But now she forced herself to focus on him again, finding his handsome face creased with concern.

"Are you okay? Evie Lee asked you to help her with that ribbon three times now."

"Oh," Jenn said. Then, working to regain her equilibrium, she added, "I'm sorry."

"But are you okay?" Matt repeated.

"I'm fine."

She must not have been very convincing because her answer only made him look at her quizzically, as if he wasn't sure what was wrong with her but still believed something was.

Then he said, "We're about done here. Maybe you ought to rest up for the hour till suppertime. You don't want to be tuckered out for tonight's concert in town."

Ordinarily Jenn wouldn't have welcomed any suggestion that prematurely ended her time with him. But with that number burning a hole in her pocket she lied and said maybe she was slightly tired and ought to go lie down.

She left Evie Lee and Matt, feeling Matt's eyes on her the whole way out of the den and hating the guilt she took with her.

But she felt more and more strongly that she shouldn't tell him about the phone number until she knew what it might unveil.

She just went to her rooms and closed the door behind her. But resting was the last thing on her mind. Instead she pulled the scrap of wrapping paper out of her pocket and rushed to the phone on the bedside table.

Once she got there a wave of uneasiness stalled her. A wave of uneasiness that came from the sudden thought that everything could change by just dialing that number...

You could just not do it, she told herself. You could throw away the paper and hope you forget the number again.

But she knew she couldn't do that. She couldn't ignore the first thing she'd actually remembered that wasn't some bit of meaningless trivia. She had to dial that number and find out where it led.

So she took a deep breath, sighed it out, picked up the receiver and dialed, not breathing at all through the two rings that sounded before an answering machine ended them.

"Hi. You've reached Greta's machine. Leave a message at the beep."

Greta?

The beep sounded and Jenn almost didn't speak. She didn't know what to say and for a split second she considered just hanging up.

Then, in a hurry, she said, "This is Jenn Johnson and I—"

"Jenn?" a woman's voice said, breaking in.

"Yes, this is Jenn. Jenn Johnson."

"Of course it's Jenn Johnson. What other Jenn would it be? Where have you been? I've been worried sick about you. Why didn't you let me know when you got where you were going?"

There were a lot of questions in that outpouring and Jenn wasn't too sure which of them to address first. She opted for the one that struck the sharpest note with her. "Where *was* I going?"

"Where were you going?" the woman countered as if it were a dumb question. "How would I know when you wouldn't tell me? You just said you'd call me Tuesday night when you got there—wherever *there* was—to let me know you'd arrived safe and sound." She paused a moment then said, "What do you mean where were you going?"

Suspicion laced her tone and Jenn could tell this Greta person—if that's who she was—had caught on that something was amiss.

"It's kind of complicated," Jenn answered. "I know this will sound strange, but do you recognize my voice and is Jenn Johnson familiar enough to you to be sure that's who I am?"

"Yes, I recognize your voice and I'm familiar enough with you to be sure that's who you are. What's going on?"

"It'll sound crazy," Jenn warned.

"Too late. This already sounds crazy."

"Are you the Greta whose machine I reached?"

"You know I am. You've known me forever."

"I'm sorry, but Greta what?"

"Greta what? You mean, like what's my last name?"

"Yes."

"Is this a joke?"

"I wish it were."

"Greta Banks. I'm your best friend, remember?"

"No. That's the problem. I don't remember anything." Jenn went on to explain her amnesia along with what had happened to her and the fact that she was in Wyoming.

"You've got to be kidding," Greta said when Jenn had finished.

"It's no joke and I'm not kidding. We haven't had any luck finding out much about me. But this phone number—your phone number—just came back to me a few minutes ago out of the blue so I thought I'd dial it and see what came of it."

"My gosh," Greta said in a stunned sigh. "Are you all right?"

"Physically I'm fine. Even the bump on my head is nearly gone. But so far your phone number is the only thing I've remembered."

"Maybe because you've called it about a million times."

"Could you tell me what you know about me?"

The woman on the other end of the line laughed slightly. "This is just too weird. I know everything about you. Except what's going on with this trip."

"Could you tell me some of it?" Jenn reiterated.

"Like, what do you want to know? Everything from the sixth grade on when we met or more recent things?"

"More recent things. Like where do I live and work? Am I married? Or separated or divorced? Do I have kids? Do I have parents or brothers or sisters? That kind of thing. The basics."

Greta took another deep breath before she plunged in. "Well, up until a year ago you were a history professor at the Denver branch of the University of Colorado. But you left your job to take care of your grandmother. She was your only living relative. Your parents and brother were killed in a car accident when you were eleven, and you came from Kansas to live with your grandmother. That's when we met.''

''What was wrong with my grandmother that she needed taking care of?''

''She had liver cancer,'' Greta said gently. ''She died about two weeks ago.''

The old woman in the dream—was it possible that was her grandmother rather than her?

''I must have been very close to her,'' Jenn said, searching for memories and finding only a muted kind of pain that didn't seem to belong to anything she could put her finger on.

''You were very close. You loved her dearly. You still lived with her, in fact,'' Greta informed.

Jenn repeated the address on her driver's license and said, ''Is that where we lived? Because I found out that there was no house there anymore.''

''About the time your grandmother had to be hospitalized, the city bought out all the houses in the area. When you weren't at the hospital with your grandmother—which was most of the time—you stayed with me rather than trying to find another place. And since her death you've been here.''

''So I'm not married or living with a man or involved with a man I might have stayed with?''

''No. You've never been married. There was a guy—Barry—who you were pretty serious about. But he didn't like it when you started spending less time with him and more with your grandmother. He gave you an ultimatum—put her in a nursing home or things were over between you two. You decided if he was that selfish you didn't want him. There hasn't been anyone since then.''

''I imagine that means I don't have any kids, either,'' Jenn said, just wanting that confirmed, too.

''No, you don't have any kids. This is so weird.''

''I know. For me, too. What about money?'' Jenn asked. ''Do I have much of it?''

Greta laughed a little wryly. ''You've been struggling. You didn't make that much in your job and it hasn't paid anything since you took sabbatical. You've lived on your savings until it ran out a few weeks ago. Plus the medical bills ate up everything your grandmother had.''

''Did I have maybe about two thousand dollars left from something?''

''Two thousand dollars? No. You'll have some money from the sale of the house you and your grandmother shared when it gets through probate, but for now you're broke, kiddo. You're going back to work in January when the next semester starts but until then... Well, we've just been making ends meet.''

We... Meaning Greta had been supporting them both. But Jenn could tell that the other woman was too good a friend to make it sound as if Jenn had been her charity case, which she apparently had been.

Then Greta said, ''Do you need two thousand dollars? Are you in some kind of trouble? Is that what it'll cost to get your car dug out? Or is that for medical bills?''

Jenn appreciated the compassion in the other woman's tone. And the sense she conveyed that if Jenn needed money she'd do what she could to help.

"No. I don't need any money. But could money have been the reason I went on this trip? Maybe I was going to see a relative to borrow it so I'd have something to tide me over until I'm back at work?''

"You don't have any relatives. I told you, there was just you and your grandmother. And I don't see how this trip could have had anything to do with going somewhere to get money, unless you were trying to find the pot at the end of the rainbow. Last week you just said there was something you had to do and you were going to have to take a trip to do it. The cheapest way was to drive but you had to charge the gas on your credit card because you didn't even have enough cash to fill the tank.''

"And I didn't tell you where I was going or why?''

"No. I couldn't figure it out. You've never *not* told me anything. But it was like something about this was a big secret or something. You just wouldn't say. And now you're in Wyoming?''

"Yes.''

"You wouldn't happen to be in a place called Elk Creek, would you?''

"Yes. Do you know it?''

"No, but I'm not surprised. Your grandmother subscribed to a newspaper from there for all the years I've known you and you always read the thing front to back. You talked about the town and the people in it and you knew the strangest things, every little detail about everything. I guess when there isn't a lot of news to write about they put in all the gossipy little tidbits and every ounce of minutiae. But you've never been there so maybe you just decided to finally see it for yourself. Except I don't know why you wouldn't tell me that.''

"Why did my grandmother subscribe to a newspaper from here?''

"She wouldn't say. In fact, she read the newspaper but wouldn't talk about any of it. That was what got you so curious. You started to read it to try to figure out why she got it, to see if you could tell what she might be looking for in it or what about it interested her. Then you got hooked, as if it were a series of novels you just couldn't wait for the next installment to. You sort of had a fantasy about going there someday, having a simpler life, living in a small town.''

"And I paid so much attention to what I read in the newspaper that it was like I got to know the people I read about—like familiar characters in a book. Plus there were probably pictures, which means I got to know how those people looked, too,'' Jenn said, only guessing because none of what Greta had told her actually sparked any memory. But the newspaper seemed like the likeliest explanation for how she knew so much about Elk Creek's citizens.

"Sometimes you talked about what you'd read as if the people in the newspaper were old friends or family or something, yeah. But what I don't understand is why, all of a sudden, you just had to go there and then wouldn't even tell me.''

Or that she had $2157 to take with her...

But Jenn didn't say that. If Greta—who was her best friend since they were kids and who knew everything else about her—didn't know about that money, it *must* be bad.

''Am I an honest person? A good person?'' Jenn ventured, worrying that if she had over two thousand dollars and she'd let Greta believe she was broke so Greta would foot the bills it didn't bode well for her character.

But Greta only laughed. ''What a dumb question. You're Miss Straight-As-An-Arrow.''

''Have you ever known me to steal anything?''

''Steal anything? You? Jenn, I keep a jar of quarters in the cupboard to use when I do laundry. You wouldn't even touch them to do your own laundry without asking first and then keeping a running total to pay me back. A quarter, Jenn, you wouldn't even take a quarter that wasn't yours.''

Then where did that $2157 come from?

''Did you ever think I might have a secret life?''

Again Greta laughed. ''A secret life. I even know when you have PMS every month. You don't have a secret life. You're so open about everything it isn't funny. This trip is the only thing in the world you wouldn't tell me about. But now that I know Elk Creek is where you were going it's probably because you thought I'd think you'd lost your mind a little with the grief over your grandmother if you were actually going to some place you've just been day-dreaming about forever.''

Somehow Jenn didn't think coming to Elk Creek had been merely chasing a fantasy. Although she had no idea what other reason there could have been.

"Listen," Greta said then. "Do you think I could get there by train? The roads are bad and all the newscasts are warning people not to drive unless it's absolutely necessary. But if I could get to you by train—''

"No," Jenn answered, cutting Greta off before she got any further. "I don't think the train is running, either. Elk Creek is snowed in. Besides, what would you do here?''

"I just hate the thought of you being all alone up there, knowing no one and not even being able to remember your own name.''

"That sounds a lot worse than it is. The Mc-Dermots are being very kind and I'm staying in their beautiful home. I'll be all right for a while.''

"But when the weather clears I'll come up there and at least drive home with you. Otherwise how will you find your way back?''

That was a good point. But at that moment Jenn had enough to digest, she didn't even want to think about leaving Matt on top of everything else. Not yet anyway.

"There's still hope that my memory will come back," Jenn pointed out. "Maybe remembering your phone number was just the first step. Maybe that means things will start to break through. Even if it's only in bits and pieces, it's something."

"But what if it doesn't? Maybe a doctor down here would know more about how to help you."

"The doctor here is good. I'm sure if there was anything that could be done he'd do it."

"And in the meantime you just have to stay up there, with strangers, probably all through Christmas?"

"It's okay," Jenn said, consoling her friend who made that prospect sound like punishment. "Really," she added, thinking that Greta had no way of knowing just how much being there with Matt was *not* punishment.

"Give me the number there so I can at least reach you," Greta said then.

That made Jenn pause.

It was a logical, reasonable suggestion. But Matt didn't know she'd been going to make this call and at that moment all Jenn could think of was how she'd explain a phone call from her best friend in Denver if it happened before she told him.

"I think it's better if I call you," Jenn hedged.

"You don't want me to call you there?" Greta sounded confused. And maybe a little hurt.

"It's just that this whole thing is complicated and…" And she didn't know why she felt so strange about everything. But she did. "I just want some time to work this all out myself. In my head. To maybe try using what you've told me to nudge my memory out of hiding. I may not tell anyone here about coming up with your phone number or talking to you until I can see if it spurs more.''

"You act like you don't believe what I've told you and so you don't want to repeat it until you can be sure.''

Jenn hadn't realized it before, but there was something to that.

"I think that's part of it. Not that I don't believe you. It's just that... Well, it still doesn't feel like me. I want to sit with the idea of it all for a little while, I guess. Before I tell anyone.''

"It isn't as if I've told you something you have to be ashamed of.''

But she also hadn't been able to tell her anything about that money, either, and there could still be something terrible tied up in that.

"I know. It's just...I just can't tell you how odd this whole thing is. And until I know more or feel more comfortable with it, I may keep it to myself.''

"Okay,'' Greta said, agreeing but clearly not understanding. "Will you call and check in with me so I know you're okay?''

"Sure,'' Jenn promised.

"And you're positive you're all right?''

"Everything but my memory is fine. Great, in fact. I feel great.''

"This is so strange, Jenn.''

"That you *don't* have to tell me.''

"You aren't being held captive by some creep or something, are you?''

"No,'' Jenn answered with a laugh, unable to even imagine Matt McDermot as a creep. "The

McDermots couldn't be nicer people.'' And one of them in particular.

''And you really don't know if there's some purpose to your going up to that small town in the first place?''

''No, I don't.''

''Is there somebody you think you went to see?''

''I don't know. I've met a lot of people but no one sparks any memory.'' Any memory about her at any rate.

''And there's nothing we can do but sit tight until the roads clear?'' Greta reiterated.

''Nothing,'' Jenn confirmed.

Neither of them said anything for a moment.

Then Greta said, ''I hate to hang up. I feel like you're adrift and I want to be there with you.''

''It's okay. Honestly.''

''But you'll call me.''

''I'll call you. But I should hang up now.''

Greta didn't respond to that right away, but eventually she said, ''Okay. I'll keep a good thought.''

''Thanks. And thanks for the information.''

They said goodbye and Jenn finally replaced the receiver on the hook, staring at the phone as if that would make what Greta Banks had just told her seem more real.

It didn't, though.

And Jenn was left debating about how—and when—to tell Matt what she'd just found out about herself.

Chapter Ten

There was no rest for Jenn during what remained of that hour until suppertime. Instead her mind raced with the information she'd just garnered from her phone call to Greta Banks.

Greta Banks. Her best friend since childhood.

And Jenn had had a grandmother who'd died two weeks ago.

And a job as a history professor.

All of it was news to Jenn.

And none of it had inspired a single drop of memory. There was still a complete blackout in her brain. She couldn't even be sure if the old woman in her dreams *was* her grandmother or if it was just herself as an old woman the way it had seemed to her before.

Her grandmother…

The grandmother who had raised her for the second half of her growing-up years. The grandmother she'd loved so much she'd lived with her into adulthood. The grandmother she'd cared for to the end of her life, buried and no doubt mourned deeply.

Yet all Jenn could find in herself was that vague spot of pain that she couldn't actually put her finger on.

She got up from where she was still sitting on the bed, too near that telephone that had just complicated things for her, and went to the closet to choose something to wear to the Christmas concert Matt was taking her to in town after dinner.

No kids. No husband. No boyfriend. No entanglements at all, she thought along the way.

That was good to know, at least.

It was good to know she hadn't left behind anyone—but Greta—who had been needlessly worrying about her. Anyone she had to run back to. Anyone she was being unfaithful to.

Which meant that her attraction to Matt wasn't doing anyone any harm.

Except that she wasn't actually convinced of that.

But why not?

Maybe because until she knew everything there was to know about herself, she couldn't be sure that there wasn't something that could rear its ugly head and do damage.

Something about that *money* that could still rear its ugly head and do damage, she thought as she chose a cropped chenille turtleneck and a pair of warm wool slacks.

The money had to be the key, she decided, because thoughts of letting Matt know she'd remembered Greta's phone number and called to find out what she now knew about herself made her feel exactly the way thoughts of that money in the shaving kit made her feel. Bad. As if it could ruin everything.

She didn't understand it. There wasn't anything in what Greta had told her that was damning or shameful, but there it was. She couldn't shake the sense that to reveal what she'd learned in the call to Greta, to reveal that she had the money, would make everything come crashing down on her head.

Of course she didn't know what *everything* was, but that was how she felt.

So what *was* she going to do about telling Matt? she asked herself.

The answer seemed clear.

She wasn't going to rush into it.

She'd tell him eventually, of course. There was no doubt about that. She just didn't want to tell him now.

For now she just wanted to keep everything to herself. The way she'd been keeping the existence of the money to herself.

She wanted to mull over what Greta had told her. She wanted to use it to jog her memory, to coax it back to life. She wanted to wait until she somehow knew exactly what was going on with her and with that money and could present Matt with the full story—without any holes, without any ambiguities, without any qualms.

As things were at that moment, with the information she had and the lingering sense of something ominous in the wind over that money, she definitely had qualms.

In a way, not coming clean with Matt until she knew more might act as an incentive to get her memory back.

She swore she'd work harder at it from that moment on so that before too long she could tell him everything at once.

She just hoped that when she knew the whole story it was one she *could* tell without qualms.

The Christmas concert was held at the church and given by the church choir. There was no service, just the music—traditional religious and pop carols all sung by the townsfolk who comprised the choir.

They stood on risers in front of the altar and were accompanied by a small orchestra, also made up of townsfolk. The orchestra, seated in folding chairs at the base of the risers, wasn't quite as good as the choir but no one commented on the missed notes and chords when they happened.

The church was left dark except for the flames of candles burning atop tall candelabra that rose along either side of the chancel. It made for an intimate ambience as Jenn sat beside Matt with what seemed like the remainder of Elk Creek's citizens crowded into every pew and standing along the walls, across the rear of the church and all the way into the entry.

It was a wonderfully lively concert, infused with enthusiasm and rife with Yule spirit right up to the end.

And that end came with the announcement that the "Hallelujah Chorus" would be the final song and that the choir invited everyone to join in.

Copies of the sheet music were handed out to the audience, and it made for a powerful conclusion as almost everyone, including Matt and Jenn, took part.

As she sang, Jenn realized that her voice wasn't half-bad. But more than her own voice she enjoyed the booming tenor of Matt's from beside her.

But then what about Matt *didn't* she enjoy?

He'd changed clothes just before leaving the ranch, too, putting on a black Western shirt over a silver-gray mock turtleneck that accentuated the thick strength of his neck. He'd also put on a pair of tight black jeans that left nothing to the imagination in the way of massive thighs, narrow hips and a tremendous derriere Jenn had gotten a glimpse of as he'd shrugged out of his coat when they'd taken their seats in the church.

He'd shaved for the second time that day, too, so the heady scent of his aftershave had wafted to Jenn all through the ride in the truck into town and during the concert, too.

And as the "Hallelujah Chorus" drew to its end, she sneaked yet another sideways peek at his gorgeous profile, amused by the vigor he was putting into the climactic conclusion of the song. The man even had great ears, she thought, and she had an inexplicable urge to run her hand over the golden-brown spikes of his hair on top.

She refrained, though, instead contenting herself with his thigh running the length of hers and her arm tucked slightly behind his on the crowded pew.

The ''Hallelujah Chorus'' culminated in a burst of applause that brought everyone to their feet as the choir took a bow and the entertainment portion of the evening concluded.

Then the choir director invited all of the audience to partake of the Christmas cookies and punch being served in the church basement.

Jenn and Matt filed downstairs with the rest of the celebrants, amid the noise of mingled voices and laughter as everyone seemed to be enjoying themselves as much as Jenn was.

But her enjoyment was muted when the same thing happened that had happened every other time she'd been in town: She was the main attraction once she and Matt were in the basement as folks she hadn't yet met were eager to hear what she knew about them.

It wasn't that she didn't like Ally and Jackson Heller and meeting Ally's daughter Meggie and seeing their new infant son. It wasn't that she was unhappy to recognize Beth and Ash Blackwolf, whose baby boy and toddler daughter were adorable. It wasn't that she had anything but good feelings toward Savannah and Clint Culhane who had just announced that Savannah was pregnant. It wasn't that she felt anything but friendly toward Ivy and Cully

Culhane whose two daughters and new son were also beautiful.

It was just that now that Jenn knew how she'd come by the information about them all she felt sort of a fraud. Like someone who'd studied intensely for an exam and then pretended she'd just come by her vast knowledge naturally.

But what could she do? She hated to disappoint people who were all so warm and kind. And she couldn't confess to how she'd come by the information even though now she knew it must have been from reading Elk Creek's newspaper.

So she could only try to downplay what still seemed like a phenomenon to everyone else, hoping to deflect some of the limelight.

Luckily Matt seemed to notice her lack of enthusiasm because not long after they'd sampled a few cookies and sipped some punch, he leaned in close enough to her ear so that only Jenn could hear him and said, "This is wearing thin tonight, isn't it? How about a walk across to the town square to see the lights? Just you and me."

Jenn could have kissed him.

Well, there really wasn't a moment she was with him that she *wouldn't* have liked to kiss him, but at that particular moment she was especially grateful for the reprieve.

"That sounds great," she whispered back.

As she smiled up at him, she was struck all over again by how incredibly, ruggedly good-looking he was. It set off a little skitter of delight inside her to know she was about to get a few minutes alone with him—the first she'd had that day, since they'd wrapped packages with Evie Lee and had Buzz in the truck with them for the drive into town.

Matt made a show of dragging her away from the crowd to have her to himself then and before too long they both had on their coats and gloves again and were stepping out into the crisp night air.

Delicate flakes of snow fell like stardust glistening in the glow of Victorian streetlights as Matt took Jenn's hand and they crossed the street to the town square, sending a little stardust sparkling inside her, too.

She knew he was only making sure she didn't slip and fall on the icy road but still she had hopes that he wouldn't let go once they reached the other side where the cobbled walkways had been shoveled and salted.

He did, though. He let go of her the moment she was on safer ground.

She told herself it was for the best. That that was what he should have done because things between them needed to be kept cool.

But it didn't help. The truth was, all she really wanted was that big hand of his encasing hers regardless of what she knew they *should* do.

She took a deep breath of the frigid air and sighed it out as if clearing her lungs when in fact she was trying to clear her yearnings, and focused her attention on the Christmas decorations they were walking through.

Every tree in the square—evergreens and bare-branched elms and oaks and maples—had brightly colored lights artfully entwined in their outstretched limbs. Among the trees were white wire sculptures of a Santa-and-gift-bearing sleigh with eight reindeer just beginning to lift off from the ground behind the ninth, red-nosed reindeer in front. There were also snowmen in top hats, two eight-foot dancing bears, and frolicking and grazing deer here and there, all leading to the huge gazebo in the middle of the square.

The gazebo was completely outlined in tiny white lights, setting it aglow. Large, white-lit balls hung from its eaves between red ribbon-wound posts all the way around.

Another Christmas tree—this one cut—stood displayed in the center of the gazebo. It was decorated not only with lights but with ornaments, too, each one a contribution from the folks and families of Elk Creek.

"Wow!" Jenn said when she'd taken it all in, as Matt led her up into the gazebo to see the tree. "This is just beautiful, isn't it?"

"Mmm," he said but in such a way that Jenn's curiosity made her glance at him.

She found he wasn't looking at any of the Christmas decorations. Instead he was looking at her with eyes so warm they heated her as surely as any furnace.

But she tried to ignore it, reminding herself that it was Matt who had released her hand when she would have let him keep it.

So instead of continuing to look up into those

great green eyes, she glanced away at the ornaments and pretended she hadn't caught the compliment.

"Is one of these yours?" she asked, nodding at the ornaments that each had a name somewhere on them.

"No, not mine specifically. But there's a Mc-Dermot ornament. Let's see… I think we're facing the courthouse, if I remember right," he said, getting his bearings and then scanning ornaments until he found it.

"There it is," he said victoriously, pointing to a miniature snow globe surrounding an intricately detailed scene of Santa's North Pole, complete with elves and Santa himself.

"Very nice," Jenn complimented.

They studied the rest, laughing over many of them and what they symbolized for the givers. A porcelain teddy bear, for instance, had come from Junebug Brimley, the McDermot's three-hundred-pound housekeeper. Word around town was that it was in honor of the teddy bear all six of her now-grown, strapping sons had carried as children. It was something her sons were widely teased about, Matt informed Jenn.

Margie Wilson, who owned Margie Wilson's Café, had contributed tiny copper pots and pans hanging from a red ribbon. Jackson Heller had hung a miniature helicopter that was an exact replica of the larger version he owned. There were several horses and a few cows—no avoiding ranchers' admiration of those—and there was a fair share of ornaments that neither Matt nor Jenn could figure out, so for those they made up stories—most of them silly—to explain them.

"I can't believe you didn't come up with an ornament of your own so you could be a part of the traditions of your new hometown," Jenn said when they'd made their way around the whole tree.

Matt went to sit on the seat that lined the perimeter of the gazebo, stretching out his long legs to cross at the ankles and letting both arms run along the upper shelf of the bench seat's back. "Are you thinkin' of me as a dog again and suggestin' I mark out some territory?" he joked.

"No, that's not what I meant," she answered, unable to keep her eyes off the sexy T he'd formed with his lean, muscular body. "I'm just saying it would have been like a sign to let people know you're here to stay and want to be included in the community."

"And what would you have me hang up there? A pair of spurs?"

"That would work. If spurs have some special meaning for you."

"Oh, now it not only has to give the message that I'm here to stay, it has to have a special meaning, too. Like what?"

"You just have to put your mind to it. Think of something that has to do with a momentous occasion in your life."

That didn't seem to require much effort because almost instantly his mouth stretched into a cat-that-ate-the-canary smile. "I could put up a red-and-white stocking cap," he said.

"Which would signify…"

"The red-and-white stocking cap I wore for three months after Bax shaved my head while I was sleeping. I was thirteen."

"Why did he do that?"

"Just out of orneriness. And because I'd sneaked into his room the night before and done some doodling on his back with a black marker that had made him a laughingstock in the locker room."

"So you deserved it."

"Well, he'd stolen all my underwear before that and I'd had to go around without any for two days. Then all those little tighty-whities just happened to avalanche out of my locker at a very inopportune moment."

"So *he* deserved it."

"Well, he was gettin' even for my tellin' a bunch of his friends that his favorite toy had been a doll until he was three."

"Why do I think this could go all the way back to birth?"

"Nah, we didn't start causin' each other trouble until we were in junior high. But it was pretty much ongoing from then."

If the contented smile on his face was any indication, he was enjoying the memories.

Then he said, "Or we could hang up a little blue Volkswagen ornament. The Beetle was my first car."

Jenn let her gaze travel from mile-wide shoulders all the way down the length of legs that seemed to go on forever, trying to picture him driving such a small vehicle. "You must have been shorter when you were sixteen. Or did you have to drive with your knees under your chin?"

"I managed a whole lot more than just drivin' in that car," he said with a wicked grin.

"Let me guess—you lost your virginity in it, too?"

"One balmy night in July," he confirmed.

"Did you have company or were you by yourself?" she goaded.

That made him laugh. "I beg your pardon," he said in mock offense. Then he said, "Lily Bell," with a wistfulness in his voice.

But Jenn could tell he was only putting it on for her benefit.

"Maybe you should hang a bell on the tree, then," she suggested, refusing to show the jealousy he was trying to taunt her into, even though she felt a twinge of it.

"I could," he said as if considering it seriously. "'Course it'd probably be a dead giveaway even up here. I think Lily's reputation crossed state lines."

"I'll bet. Maybe you should stick with the car."

"The Love Bug, that's what I called 'er."

"The car or Lily?"

"The car."

Jenn rolled her eyes. "You and every other boy with a Volkswagen."

His grin turned wry. "Gettin' back some memories of your own?"

"Just a good guess."

"Maybe I should look for a Zorro ornament," he

suggested then. "Rescuer of damsels in distress. And he had that nifty sword."

"Nifty?" Jenn repeated, laughing.

"Nifty," he confirmed, lunging to his feet, hopping onto the bench seat and slashing a *Z* into the air with an imaginary sword just before he swooped down on her and spun her around in circles until she was dizzy and laughing and wanting to fall into his arms.

She didn't get the chance, though, because he spun her right onto the bench seat and pretended to mark her with another *Z* as his grand finale.

"Be careful about makin' fun of Zorro," he advised as he took a step up onto the seat and sat on the back ledge so that she was sitting beside his feet.

"I'll try to keep that in mind," she assured facetiously.

Matt raised his long, straight nose into the air as if catching a scent on the wind. Then he shivered like a dog shaking off water and said, "Whose dumb idea was it to come out here when it's five below zero?"

"Yours."

"Nah, I think it was yours."

"If you're cold, we could go back."

He made a face that let her know that wasn't on his top ten list of things to do. "Or we could just go on home."

A much better plan, as far as Jenn was concerned.

"I'm game if you are," she informed him. "But what about Buzz? He rode with us. Shouldn't we take him home, too?"

"He'll just ride with somebody else when he can't find us. It isn't as if there's a shortage of people goin' back to the ranch."

"Okay. He's your grandfather," Jenn said in a way that let him know she wasn't willing to share the blame if Buzz got mad.

"What do you think he'll do to me? Take me out to the woodshed and turn me over his knee?"

"It probably isn't any more than you have coming."

"Yeah, but it'd be a struggle for him. I'm bigger than he is," Matt confided, bending far enough over to breathe a warm gust of air in her ear again.

Then he leaped off the seat, gently yanked Jenn up by her lapels and linked his elbow through hers to guide her out of the gazebo and back through the lights and decorations of the town square to where they were parked in the church lot.

And without encountering anyone to inform they were leaving, they were on their way again, slowly navigating the snow-packed road out of town.

They fell into a companionable silence as Matt concentrated on his driving, and before too long they were back at the ranch.

It was the first time since Jenn had been taken in as Matt's houseguest that the place had been empty.

"Feels kind of hollow without anybody else here," she observed as the door closing behind them seemed to echo.

"You're just gettin' used to communal livin'."

Not something she *should* get accustomed to if Greta Banks was right and she was all alone in the world. But that wasn't something Jenn wanted to start thinking about again and she pushed the thoughts aside.

Since everyone was going to be gone for the evening the heat had been turned down and the house was chilly.

Matt rubbed his hands together as if it were colder than it actually was and said, "I'm thinkin' we need a fire."

"Sounds good," Jenn agreed, hugging herself against the chill.

"If I make it in the living room or the rec room we're gonna have the whole family with us when they get back. But if we do it in my room or yours, we won't have to do any more socializin' tonight," Matt said as he hung their coats on the hall tree. "I'll leave it up to you."

"I've had enough socializing for one night," Jenn heard herself say, even as she knew it was just asking for trouble to be alone with him in front of a private fire.

But once the words were out, Matt didn't dispute the decision. "Okay. Your place or mine?" he asked with a lascivious insinuation in his voice.

Jenn ignored it. "Mine, that way I get the benefits of the fire all night to keep me warm."

"And you'd let me freeze to death?"

"Sleep with your boots on," she advised.

"You're a hard woman," he moaned as he ushered her down the hall to her rooms.

Matt made a quick fire while Jenn followed his instructions to move the coffee table out of the way and put the couch cushions on the floor in front of the sofa so they could be closer to the heat.

Then Jenn sat on one of the cushions, with her back to the base of the sofa, watching Matt nurse the flames to life.

But it wasn't the fire she was looking at.

It was Matt. In all his glory.

Tall and muscular and powerful and gorgeous.

It was heady just looking at him…

When the flames were roaring on their own, he joined her, sitting on the other cushion but at an angle that had him facing her, with one leg curved beneath him, one arm stretched behind her on the love seat, and the other leg bent at the knee to brace his remaining arm.

"A Volkswagen, huh?" she said, thinking that even folded up like that he was still a force to be reckoned with. She couldn't imagine him fitting into such a compact car to drive, much less to do more amorous things.

"Where there's a will, there's a way," he quoted as if he could tell what she was thinking.

"You must have had a big will."

He grinned. "I don't like to brag."

Jenn laughed, feeling her face flush slightly because she hadn't intended her comment to be a double entendre.

Matt was staring down at her, his spectacularly handsome face gilded by the fireglow. That sexy dimple in his chin was just a deep shadow, and every sharp angle and plane of his features was in strong relief. Jenn felt a swell of warmth wash through her that had absolutely nothing to do with the flames from the hearth.

"You know," he said in a more intimate voice. "I'm likin' havin' you around."

That made her smile.

"You know, I'm likin' bein' around," she responded, mimicking his accent.

"Are you makin' fun of me again?" he asked without the slightest tinge of offense.

"You're pretty much fun all on your own," she said, purposely misinterpreting his words and meaning what she said because she was having such a good time.

He laughed slightly and returned the compliment. "You, too."

With eyes that searched and penetrated and held hers like a tractor beam, he seemed to draw her to him so that when he leaned in to kiss her she was already halfway to meeting him, without even thinking about it.

And when their mouths met it was as if every moment since he'd kissed her last was only a prelude to kissing her again.

It didn't last nearly long enough before he ended it and went back to looking down into her eyes, searching once more for something she couldn't guess at.

He laid a callused hand gently to her cheek, stroking it with featherlight brushes of his thumb. And she didn't know what to think.

But the truth was she couldn't think about much

of anything except the soft warmth his mouth had left on hers and how much she wanted it back again.

Then he whispered, "Oh hell," as if giving in to something inevitable, and slid his hand around to her nape to pull her to him once more, kissing her with a new intensity, a new determination, and giving her what she wanted most at that moment.

His lips were parted and so were hers, and in no time at all his tongue came to say hello, too.

Jenn greeted it with her own, welcoming him, ready to play.

And play they did. Chasing games, and circle dances, and parries and thrusts that started her mind toward thoughts of more than kissing, that awakened parts of her body she knew were better off sleeping.

But it was too late. Matt's wonderfully adept mouth deepened their kisses so that they were no longer playful, so that they were filled with an ever-increasing passion that more than awakened her desires. That energized them. That fed them while still making them hungry for more.

In answer to that hunger Jenn laid her hands to the rock-solid wall of his chest, feeling the beat of his heart keeping pace with the race of hers.

She felt something else, too. The warmth of his body coming through his shirt. The strength. The power. The pure elemental sensuality that ignited those awakened, energized desires in her. That made them burn bright and intense.

Matt wrapped his free arm around her, pulling her closer. Close enough that her own arms slipped over his massive shoulders and left her palms pressed to the muscles of his back, her breasts pressed against his chest.

She hadn't even been aware of her hardened nipples until they came into contact with him. But now she knew a need even greater than before as her breasts, her nipples, ached for more. For the touch of that oh-so-capable hand still at her nape.

Couldn't he feel how much she yearned for the magic of that touch?

Maybe not. After all, there were so many layers of clothes between them.

But maybe, maybe, if she arched her spine a little...

Maybe if she massaged his back the way she was longing for him to massage her front...

But massaging his back only added fuel to the rapidly growing needs alive within her, because he had a remarkable back. A mass of solid, masculine muscle that she filled her hands with and explored until she also ached to feel it all without the hindrance of his clothes.

In fact, she ached for that so much that she couldn't resist finding her way beneath his outer shirt. The knit of the mock turtleneck he wore still impeded her, but at least she was one layer nearer.

She hadn't intended that as a message—she'd only been answering her own need for more closeness—but apparently he took it as a message just the same.

Or maybe he was only answering a need of his own, because he trailed a similar path that led his hand underneath the back of her sweater to her bare skin there.

Nice. It was so nice to finally feel flesh against flesh, even if it was only his hand against her back.

Nice enough to want more...

Jenn followed his lead and pulled that last layer of shirt from his waistband so she could slide beneath it and lay her hands to the silken heat of his back. Silk over steel. She delved into it as their kisses grew even deeper, as mouths opened wide and lost any hint of inhibition.

But still she wanted—needed—more. More of him. More from him.

And then the hand that had been bracing her head against the onslaught of his kiss began a slow descent. A slow descent that made her every craving grow with anticipation as he went from the side of her neck to her shoulder, to her collarbone, and finally—*finally*—to her breast.

Again she cursed the clothes that kept them apart, but her nipple came to attention anyway and thrust itself into his palm as a slight groan of pleasure rumbled deep in her throat.

Matt must have hated the barriers of their clothes as much as she did because almost as quickly as his hand had reached her breast, he abandoned it to slip underneath the short-cropped sweater and reclaim it from a better vantage point.

But there was still her bra separating them and Jenn regretted having worn it at all.

He made quick work of unfastening it and then that most glorious of all glorious hands was there, covering her straining breast and eliciting yet another groan of pleasure from her throat.

Jenn had no memory of anything ever having felt as incredible but she couldn't imagine that anything had.

As he kneaded and teased and taunted her nipple into a kernel of yearning, a fire lit the fuse that stretched down the core of her.

But even as every sense, every nerve ending shrieked for more, for him to slake the thirst that drove her nearly insane, there was something about him that seemed to slow. To withdraw slightly.

One last, lingering squeeze of her breast said goodbye as he pulled his hand away and out from under her sweater. One last, deep, deep kiss bid a similar farewell before he took his mouth away from hers to press smaller, more chaste kisses to her chin and the side of her neck, where he buried his head and breathed hot gusts of passion-filled air against her skin.

"Maybe this isn't somethin' we should take any farther," he said, in a voice that was raspy and ragged and almost sounded tortured.

Or maybe it only sounded tortured to her because that was how she felt.

But even in the midst of raging desire, she knew he was probably right. Now that she'd opted not to tell him what she'd found out about herself today, things between them were even more complicated than they had been before. More complicated than he realized. And she knew she shouldn't let it get more complicated still by giving in to raging desires.

"You're probably right," she forced herself to say, although it wasn't easy. In fact, it was terribly, terribly difficult when he was still kneading her back the way he'd been kneading her breast only moments before.

Maybe he'd wanted her to disagree with him, to tell him that anything this powerful between two people *should* be done. And maybe if she'd have said that, he'd have picked up where he'd left off and finished what he'd started.

Instead his sigh seemed resigned to something he hadn't been resigned to before and he sat up straight and moved away from her.

"I'm just about goin' crazy, you know?" he said.

"Because of me?"

"Because of wantin' you more than I've ever wanted anyone in my life."

"Should I say I'm sorry?" she asked, flattered but still too churned up not to want to tell him to just forget everything else and make love to her after all.

He laughed but it was wry and seemed almost painful. "No, you shouldn't say you're sorry. It isn't anything you're to blame for. It's just that there you are with that red hair and that buttermilk skin and those eyes... Damn, those eyes that are the bluest things I've ever seen... And there isn't an inch of me that doesn't want you."

So give in to it. Let's both just give in to it, she almost shouted.

But she didn't. She knew she couldn't. Not while she wasn't being completely open with him.

So instead she reminded him of what she knew

was his greatest qualm. "But we don't know enough about me."

He took another deep breath as if to gain some control. "Damn," he said to himself. Then, to her, he said, "I'd better get out of here."

He didn't move, though. At least not to leave.

He stared into her eyes a while longer and then he leaned forward from a safer distance and kissed her again, an openmouthed, hungry kiss that let her know not going through with this was no easier for him than it was for her.

Then he got to his feet. "I'll see you tomorrow," he said in a voice raw with what was going through him.

"Tomorrow," Jenn answered, barely managing to get the word out.

She heard him leave but she didn't watch him go. Instead she stayed where she was, watching the fire he'd built burning hot and alive.

And all she could think about was that he'd built an even hotter fire inside her, only to let it burn unattended, too.

Chapter Eleven

Jenn woke up the next morning with a blinding headache.

She tried to ignore it. She even took aspirin for it before she'd had breakfast. But neither the aspirin nor the dry toast she forced herself to eat in hopes that food might help numbed the throbbing pain.

By eleven o'clock Matt and the rest of the household assured her they didn't need her help getting ready for the night's Christmas Eve party and sent her back to bed to sleep the headache off.

Jenn went without much of a struggle. She was just too sick to do anything else. And she did sleep. All through the remainder of the day, waking only when someone dropped what sounded like a glass to crash to pieces not far away.

4:48 PM.

That's what it said on the clock on her night table, and Jenn's first thought was that she'd wasted all those hours she'd intended to spend helping with party preparations.

But it was her second thought that really rocked her.

She thought that she wasn't sure she was in a party mood so soon after her grandmother's death.

But more powerful than that simple thought was the realization that came with it—she remembered her grandmother. Her grandmother's death. How much she'd loved her. How much it hurt to have lost her.

And she remembered everything else, too.

Not merely the overall facts that Greta Banks had told her. But everything. Jenn genuinely remembered everything. Who she was. Where she'd come from. The people and events in her life.

Even the details about that money in the shaving kit and why she'd come to Elk Creek.

She sat up in bed, testing for any lingering pain in her head.

There wasn't any. There was only a free flow of knowledge and information about every aspect of her life, every detail, to let her know the amnesia had disappeared as completely as the headache had.

And left her with some knowledge and information she wished she *didn't* have.

Jenn leaned back against the headboard and gave herself over to all the facts that were bombarding her brain suddenly.

No, she hadn't done anything wrong or illegal to come by that money in the shaving kit. But it was no wonder it had brought her such an ominous sense every time she'd thought about it. It was definitely ill-gotten gains. Just not ill-gotten gains that she was responsible for.

But it was also not money that was going to make anyone glad she'd come with it.

Certainly not anyone in the McDermot family.

The coincidence of having ended up with exactly the people she'd come to find boggled her mind, and for a moment Jenn wondered at just how strong a hand fate had had in what was going on.

But fate or not, there wasn't a way to let the McDermots know what she now knew without alienating them.

Alienating the very people who had been so kind, so helpful, who had taken her into their home.

There was no way to reveal what she now knew without alienating Matt.

What a terrible thought that was—alienating Matt.

She couldn't help picturing it in her mind. Imagining him looking at her with disgust in those dark forest-green eyes. Imagining him turning his back on her.

The whole idea hurt Jenn more than the headache had.

A lot more.

In fact, it was nearly unbearable.

And it was certainly not the Christmas gift she wanted to give him.

The Christmas gift...

She'd be ruining everyone's Christmas, she realized, not only Matt's.

Jenn closed her eyes, wishing things hadn't taken the turn they had. And why now? she wanted to shriek. Why couldn't her memory have waited to come back?

But it hadn't and there was nothing she could do about it.

At least there was nothing she could do to hide the truth from herself.

But it occurred to her that there was one thing she could do for everyone else: She could wait to let them know she'd regained her memory.

But was that the right thing to do?

She honestly wasn't sure.

It was bad enough that she hadn't told Matt she'd remembered Greta's phone number and spoken to her. Wasn't it worse to keep the total return of her memory from him?

But again she thought about Christmas. And the Christmas Eve party the McDermots were looking so forward to, working so hard to produce. How could she demolish that?

She couldn't, she decided. She owed them at least this evening and the next day to enjoy the holiday.

In the long run it wouldn't change what she had to tell them. What she had to tell them had kept for a long time already. It could keep a while longer. A while in which the McDermots could enjoy their holiday the way they deserved to.

A while in which she could enjoy the holiday.

Okay, so yes, there was an element of selfishness

to it. But was it so bad if she got to have a little joy this Christmas? Not an untarnished joy now, but a little joy all the same?

It didn't seem like such a horrible thing.

And just as soon as the holiday was over, she'd tell everyone the whole story. The whole truth. No matter what the consequences might be.

Consequences that were likely to cost her Matt.

But until those consequences kicked in, she could at least have these next hours with him. To enjoy. To savor.

To keep with her forever as memories when the truth put an end to everything else.

The party that evening was a wonderfully festive affair. Not only was the house decorated for Christmas but the lights in the living room and dining room were kept low and candles were lit on nearly every surface to add their warm glow and the pine scents to the air.

Bright red poinsettias had been set out for a fresh touch of the holiday and soft Christmas music was playing in the background as folks made trip after trip to the buffet table in the dining room.

It was a lush feast offered there, beginning with stuffed mushroom caps and cherry peppers, pickles wrapped in cream cheese and prosciutto, blue cheese torta and crackers, and a baked brie with fresh fruit.

Once the appetizers were tasted, guests moved on to the turkeys and hams, the two kinds of white potatoes and the sweet potato soufflé. There were also grilled vegetables and homemade rolls, green salad and cranberry compote.

And if anyone had any room for dessert after all that, there were a dozen different cookies plus pumpkin, pecan and mince pies, along with a chocolate mousse topped with raspberry sauce.

Jenn didn't have much of an appetite despite the appeal of all that food. But it was probably for the best, because the dress Matt's sister, Kate, had loaned her for the occasion left nothing to the imagination.

It was made of a stretchy black velvet with a lace-edged neckline that angled slightly off her shoulders and dipped demurely just below her collarbone. The bodice of the dress fitted her every curve like a second skin to her waist where a wide skirt took over to fall nearly to her ankles.

She'd washed her hair and scrunched the curls to a frenzy, leaving them free about her bare shoulders, and applied a hint-more-than-usual blush and mascara for the evening. She knew she looked as dressed up as everyone else at the party. She just hoped it was enough to hide what she feared might be reflected on her face—that she was no longer in the dark about who she was, the way she'd been every other time she'd encountered any of these people.

"How's the head holding up?"

The question came from Matt as he returned from his second trip to the buffet table to reclaim the seat next to her.

He hadn't ventured far from her side all evening

and about every half hour he inquired about her health, always by leaning in close to her ear so she could feel the warmth of his breath and smell the scent of his aftershave. Every time he did, little shivers of delight danced along her spine and they were hard to ignore.

But his phrasing of the question now about how her head was holding up made her think that holding her head up wasn't all that easy when she knew she was concealing things from him.

"Fine," she answered anyway. "I'm fine."

"You aren't eating," he observed, poking his dimpled chin toward the plate in her lap.

Jenn glanced at her dish and then at Matt.

She just wasn't hungry. Not for food at any rate. But the sight of him was definitely something she liked dining on.

He was dressed up for the occasion, too. Not formally. But he had on a white banded-collar shirt with a red-and-black Aztec design striped across the breadth of his chest, and a pair of tight black jeans that made it difficult for Jenn to keep her eyes off his derriere every time he turned around.

"Don't you like the food?" he added.

"The food's great," she answered. "But my appetite isn't."

His brows pulled together over the bridge of his long, thin nose. "Are you sure you feel okay?"

Jenn laughed. "Right as rain. I'm just not hungry."

"In that case…" Matt said, plucking an olive off her plate and popping it into his mouth.

An enormous mountain of a woman came up to them just then, giving Matt a hard time about his shirt and how he'd better not spill anything on it or he'd have hell to pay when she washed and ironed it.

Matt laughed off the reprimand and introduced the two women.

"Jenn, this is the infamous Junebug Brimley," he announced with affection. "She's usually the sole person to keep things afloat around here but first she was snowbound and then her vacation started— that's why you haven't had the pleasure of meeting her before. Junebug, the also infamous Jenn Johnson."

Jenn and the three-hundred-pound housekeeper exchanged greetings and pleasantries before Jenn said, "And if I'm not mistaken, you have six sons."

"I always liked round numbers," Junebug answered with a chuckle of pride. "Only five of 'em are here tonight, though."

"Want to see if you can pick them out?" Matt asked.

Jenn's ability to recognize strangers was once again being showcased tonight and she played along, knowing clearly now that the information came from years of poring over every single inch of print and studying every picture in every Elk Creek newspaper that had ever come to her grandmother. Greta had been right, Jenn had fantasized about the small town and being a part of it. To such an extent that she had felt as if she knew these people even before she'd arrived.

She hardly needed to think about it to recall a photograph of the whole Brimley family in an announcement of Junebug's fortieth wedding anniversary several years earlier. So she scanned the guests until she could pick out all five of the Brimley sons, each one big and brawny and so distinctively handsome they would have stood out in any crowd.

"That's them all right," Junebug confirmed when Jenn was finished. "You're as amazin' as everybody's been saying you are."

That made Jenn blush. And feel guilty all over again for deceiving these people.

"Not amazing. It's just some mental blip," she said to deflect the praise that made her uncomfortable.

One of Junebug's sons caught the older woman's eye and motioned for her to join him, so she excused herself.

But within moments Margie Wilson took her place for the same purpose.

Most of the evening went that way as anyone Jenn hadn't yet met wanted to test her ability. It seemed to be the entertainment of the party and Jenn played along because she didn't want to seem standoffish.

And in the process she tried hard not to feel like the biggest fraud to ever come to town. Not an easy task.

The party lasted until just before midnight when everyone bid the last merry Christmas and happy holidays and left.

Cleanup was being done by a crew of high-school kids who had agreed to come in at the crack of dawn to earn the substantial wage offered for their trouble on Christmas morning. But all the food had to be put away before then.

The McDermots drew straws to see who got stuck doing that and Matt pulled the short straw.

"That's okay," he said, losing gracefully. "I'll just twist Jenn's arm and make her help. She ought to be all rested up after sleepin' all day to get out of work."

"I beg your pardon." She pretended affront when in fact she was more than happy to be left alone with him.

"You didn't fool us with that headache. We knew you were only playin' possum."

If only he really did know to what extent she was playing possum...

But she just went along with his game. "I guess if you've seen through me, I'll have to make it up by helping you now."

He bent low to her ear and said, "Good choice."

Everyone else headed to bed then, and Matt barked a mock "Get busy" order as if Jenn were dawdling, setting them both into motion much as they had on cleanup duty after trimming the Christmas tree.

But food detail mainly just involved wrapping the platters of leftovers and storing them in the refrigerator. It didn't take long. In fact it didn't take long enough because when it was finished Jenn still hadn't had her fill of Matt.

"Are you tired yet?" he asked then, sounding as if he had an ulterior motive.

"Why? Do you want me to vacuum or something?" she joked.

"I was thinkin' more along the lines of a nightcap. We can watch for Santa."

"I thought the plan was for Santa to leave the kids' gifts under the trees in their parents' rooms and only family gifts were to be under the main tree in the living room."

"You never know," Matt said with an arch of an eyebrow. "Could be Santa'll make a visit to your room. If you're a good girl."

"Do good girls drink nightcaps in their rooms with men?" she joked as if it were something scandalous.

"They wouldn't be any good if they didn't," he said, sounding like a cartoon lecher.

He poured two small glasses of brandy and motioned for Jenn to precede him.

"Where to?" she asked.

"Your room," he answered without having to think about it.

Hmm... Was she mistaken or did he have something up his sleeve?

She didn't voice her curiosity, though. She just led the way.

But Jenn had only to step through the door to her sitting room to have that curiosity satisfied.

The room was warmed by a fire roaring in the fireplace. Beside it was a Christmas tree, fully decorated and lit up with bright lights. And beneath the Christmas tree was a gaily wrapped package the size and shape of a brick.

"Oh, too late," Matt pretended to lament from behind her. "Santa's already been here."

"When did you do this?" she asked, thrilled by his surprise.

"I didn't do anything. Must have been Santa's elves."

They crossed the room to the tree so Jenn could admire it, trying all the while not to pay too much attention to the present underneath it.

But Matt wasn't having any of that. He pointed to it and said, "I'll bet Santa wanted you to open that tonight."

"Oh, I don't know about that. I thought Santa's gifts were always supposed to be opened on Christmas morning."

"Check the clock. It's half past twelve—that's Christmas morning."

"Okay," she conceded. "But wait just one minute." She left him, going into her bedroom where she took another small gift out of a drawer and brought it back with her.

"Looks like Santa hid a little something for you in the other room."

Matt had moved the package to the coffee table and was sitting on the love seat waiting for her.

Jenn joined him there, holding out the present she'd managed to get with the help of his family and the owner of Elk Creek's general store.

"Don't get your hopes up," she cautioned. "It isn't anything remarkable."

He set his brandy on the coffee table and accepted the box. Then he handed her hers.

Jenn also abandoned her brandy in exchange for the gift.

But it wasn't anywhere near as heavy as a brick. In fact it was almost weightless.

"Shall we open them together or take turns?" Matt asked.

"You first," she ordered.

"Uh-uh. If we're taking turns, you first."

She was too eager to argue and so unwrapped the small package in her lap, being careful with the ribbon and paper when what she really wanted was to rip it open.

It definitely wasn't a brick. It was a small box inside a larger box. And within the smaller box was a diamond tennis bracelet.

"Oh, dear," Jenn breathed as she removed it from its nest of satin.

It was beautiful. Exquisite in fact. But very extravagant by Jenn's standards.

"This is too much," she said.

"There's method to the madness. Turn it over," Matt advised reasonably.

Jenn did as she was told, finding the bracelet engraved with his name, phone number and Elk Creek, Wyoming.

"It's only a loaner?" she guessed.

Matt laughed. "No, it's all yours. I just thought if you go out and get lost from here whoever finds you next can give me a call so I can come get you. Or if you forget about me, it will remind you."

As if she would ever forget this man who had

found her on a deserted country road and then found his way into her heart.

For some reason she didn't understand, tears welled up in her eyes. Maybe they were caused simply by the gift itself. Or maybe they were caused by the thoughtfully humorous intent in the engraving. Or maybe it was caused by the knowledge that what she was keeping secret from him would probably make *him* want to forget her.

"Thank you," she said softly, draping the bracelet over her wrist and running the fingertips of her other hand over the lustrous stones that were likely to be cold comfort when all this was over.

"My turn!" he said then, lightening the tone just that quick.

"It doesn't compare," she warned again.

"It's probably better than the measles—that's what I got the Christmas I was eight."

"But not as good as the Centerfold of the Month Calendar you got when you were fourteen," she countered. "I hear you kept it up for four years after it was outdated."

Matt raised an eyebrow. "Somebody around here's been talkin' too much."

"Mmm," she agreed. "And your all-time favorite Christmas and Christmas gift was the year you got a dog that you named Rowdy."

"Because he was," Matt confirmed reasonably. "You been checkin' up on me?"

"Just listening."

He had his package unwrapped by then and opened it, bringing out a Christmas ornament.

"Zorro. Where'd you ever find this?" he asked, holding it up to study as if it were more remarkable than it was.

"It was a fluke. I was doing some talking of my own and your sister said she'd seen this in town. I called Kansas Heller and she got it out to me. Now next year you can leave your own mark on the town Christmas tree."

"Pretty good," he said, sounding more moved by it than she'd thought he'd be.

He stood then and put it on the tree beside the fireplace, saying as he did, "Maybe the mark I want to make is on *your* Christmas tree."

Jenn set her gift and the wrapping on the coffee table about the time Matt turned her way.

"Don't you want to put it on?" he asked, nodding toward the bracelet.

"I'm afraid it'll snag the lace on the cuff of my sleeve—Kate's sleeve, I mean, since this is her dress. I'd hate to ruin it."

"Fair enough," he said, settling beside her again and stretching out one arm on the sofa behind her shoulders. But he was staring across at the Zorro ornament on her Christmas tree when he said, "I think you're wrong, though."

"About?"

"My favorite Christmas. I think it just might be this one."

He looked pointedly at her then, and once more Jenn was treated to the sight of that face that made her heart sing.

That face whose focal point were his eyes. Gorgeous green eyes that looked at her in a way that made her feel as if everything might be okay after all. As if everything just had to be.

He cupped the back of her head in the hand that was just behind it on the couch and pulled her toward him at the same time he leaned forward and pressed the sweetest of kisses to her lips.

"Merry Christmas," he whispered afterward, his face still close, his dark green eyes delving into hers.

"Merry Christmas," she whispered back, thinking that he was such an incredible man. Inside and out.

They stayed that way for a long moment as Matt seemed to study her, to contemplate something that sobered his expression.

And then he said, "I've been thinkin' a lot about last night. The truth is, I haven't been able to think about much else."

Neither had she until so many other things had crowded into her brain that afternoon.

"I've been thinkin' that maybe I know all I need to about you."

He was rubbing small circles with his thumb against her nape in a mesmerizing softness that made it difficult for Jenn to think clearly, to concentrate on what he was saying.

But as he went on she worked at it.

"I've been thinkin' that maybe what's happening between us right now is all that matters. We know you aren't married and don't have any kids so it isn't as if we're messin' up anybody else's lives. And maybe I'm willing to gamble a little with mine to have all of what we only had part of last night.''

She knew he couldn't have come to that conclusion easily.

But what about her?

The night before she'd thought that she shouldn't give in to what she wanted—making love with him—until she was honest with him. Until she wasn't keeping any secrets from him. And she was still not being honest with him, still keeping secrets from him. More in fact.

But what if she vowed to tell him everything first thing in the morning? Would it be so bad to have this one night with him now?

Maybe.

But the truth was, if she didn't have this one night with him now, *before* she told him everything, she might never have a night with him at all.

And at that moment she couldn't bear that possibility.

Just this one night, she thought. Just this one time.

''I guess I'm willing to gamble a little, too,'' she told him in a quiet voice, raising a loving hand to the side of his handsome face.

He smiled at her then. Just before he kissed her again.

That was all it took to leave behind every thought, every misgiving, every hesitation.

She cared for this man so, so much. And at that moment tasting all the fruits he'd offered the previous night was the most important thing to her. The most natural thing to her.

How could anything that important, that natural, that vital to her being at that moment, be wrong?

It couldn't. Especially when every impulse, every instinct said it was right.

So she gave herself over to that kiss that was deepening by the second as Matt's arms came around her and pulled her close, as his lips parted over hers, as his tongue came to call.

He tasted of brandy and still smelled faintly of aftershave and Jenn indulged, letting the combination go to her head.

His mouth was warm velvet, his tongue adept, and he held her in those big arms that felt as if they could move mountains.

Jenn let one of her hands rise to the side of his corded neck while the other slipped around his rib cage to his back, finding the wealth of steely muscles and deep-cut valleys that were vivid in her memories of the night before.

They went on like that for a long time. Just kissing. Mind-boggling, nerve-shattering kisses that swept Jenn up into a vortex of pure sensual awakening.

His big, agile hands found their way to her shoulders and she was grateful for the cut of that dress that left them uncovered, that left bare hands against bare skin. Gentle hands that kneaded and caressed and felt so good.

Hands that had no trouble working their way down the snug-fitting bodice to breasts that had been crying out for his touch since he'd abandoned them the night before.

And if he had worked wonders on her shoulders, what he did to her breasts was magic.

The only problem was that they weren't bare the way her shoulders were, and even though she hadn't been able to wear a bra, there was still the dress itself coming between them.

Until Matt seemed to realize just how stretchy the velvet was and that he could slide the neckline farther down her shoulders.

He didn't push it as far down as she would have liked, though. Instead he exposed only the uppermost curves of breasts that were straining to be released to his touch.

But he was more intent on teasing her.

At least that was how it seemed, because he left her that way, with just the tops of her breasts available to fingertips that traced their swell and only ventured slightly nearer nipples kerneled with neglected desires yearning for attention.

Then he lowered her neckline an inch farther, leaving it right across her nipples, tormenting her with temptation but still not reaching them.

Not until Jenn arched her back, poking those engorged globes into hands that were only toying with them in leisurely play.

He chuckled slightly, a sound that rumbled in the midst of openmouthed kisses. It was a satisfied chuckle that said he knew exactly what he was doing—he was driving her wild with wanting more.

And she *was* wild with wanting more.

But not so wild that she didn't think she could do a little driving of her own.

She pulled his shirt from his waistband, diving under it to lightly press her palms to his naked back, letting her fingertips barely skim the surface of his taut skin, sliding forward to find his own male nibs hardened into knots themselves.

Then she ran her fingertips down to his flat belly, all the way to the button on his jeans, lingering there as if she might do more, as if she might unfasten it and even go below…

But she was only teasing and instead she let her hands skitter around his waist to his back again.

That made him groan and seemed to speed things up considerably.

Down came the top of her dress, freeing her breasts not only to the air and to masterful hands, but to a mouth that suddenly abandoned hers and caught one of her breasts, one of those yearning nipples, in that warm, dark, moist cavern.

Suckling and circling, nipping and flicking, biting oh-so-gently, he drove her even more wild than his restraint had.

In fact he took her breath away with pleasure, with mounting desire and a passion that was taking her over completely.

And then he was gone.

He stopped. Everything stopped and he was up off the couch and scooping her into his arms before she knew what was happening.

He headed for her bedroom, hitting the light switch on his way out, leaving the fireglow and the lights from the Christmas tree to cast the only illumination into the bedroom.

But it was enough to show him the way to her bed.

Once he got there he didn't lay her down, though. He set her on her feet beside it and recaptured her mouth with his in a wide-open kiss that shouted of his own hunger for her.

Somewhere during the course of that kiss he slipped her dress the rest of the way down, letting it fall around her ankles where she kicked off her shoes and the bikini panties that followed it.

Jenn's focus was on his clothes then, wanting them gone, too.

She unbuttoned his shirt and smoothed it off his shoulders with hands that reveled in his taut skin along the way. Then she went a second time to the button of his waistband, opening it as she'd only let him think she might before.

His burgeoning need for her took care of the zipper, spreading it without help.

But that was where modesty got the better of Jenn and she hesitated.

Once more Matt chuckled, this time at her timidity. Then he again picked her up into his arms, laying her on the bed.

She thought that she probably should have felt embarrassed to be there, completely naked and uncovered. But it wasn't her own body she was thinking about. It was his as he shucked off his boots and socks and then pulled away his jeans while she watched.

There was no word for him but magnificent as she feasted on the sight of silky male flesh over a body sculpted by hard work. His biceps were incredible mounds of hard, honed muscle. His shoulders looked even more broad without the camouflage of clothes, his chest more massive than she'd imagined. His waist was narrow, his stomach flat, and it wasn't only his legs that were long and thick and powerful...

And then he joined her on the bed, lying beside her, one thigh across hers as his mouth came back for more urgent kisses and his hand found her breast in a glorious abandon of warm flesh against warm flesh.

Her hands explored him and every nerve ending in Jenn's body seemed electrified with the feel of him, with the feel of him touching her.

His mouth left hers yet again as he kissed a path from there down the column of her neck, into the hollow of her throat and on down the center of her chest until he reached the sensitive spot between her breasts.

Jenn's back arched of its own volition as her breasts ached for him to finally reach them with more than his hand again, with his mouth, with a return of those wonders he'd worked before.

But as he gave her what she wanted, he upped the ante with a hand that traveled lower still, that came to rest on her stomach, that inched downward until he found that spot at the juncture of her legs that was also crying out for him.

With that first impossibly soft touch of his hand she groaned. She couldn't help it.

It just felt so fantastic. Fantastic enough that she

wanted him to feel every bit as good. She wanted to touch him in the same way. More than just his back, his chest, his incredibly tight derriere.

She wanted to know him as intimately as he knew her.

So she did a slow descent of her own, finding the hot, hard staff of him and making him groan, too.

But that was about all either of them could bear.

Matt came above her then, insinuating himself between her thighs, finding his home there at the core of her. Carefully, considerately, cautiously, he entered her only by slow increments. Slower than Jenn wanted as the need to feel him inside her raged to life.

She raised her hips to help the process and, as if he knew just what she needed, he plunged fully within her, finally merging their two bodies into one.

His mouth reclaimed hers as he pushed deeply within her, as he retreated, as he pushed in again.

His tongue circled hers, lured hers, teased and tormented hers, as much in command there as he was everywhere else.

But Jenn didn't mind. She only cared about the mounting pleasure he was creating inside her. About the tiny sparks that crackled like the ends of a live wire through every square inch of her body.

In and out. In and out. Faster and faster, he carried her along. With ever increasing speed. And strength. And power. And potency. Until he couldn't go on kissing her, too. Until nothing could go on but each thrust of that monumental body into her. Until mindless passion catapulted her and something thunderous began, rumbling as if from a distance at first, but building, gaining, growing in intensity. Until lightning bolts shot through her and set off a cataclysmic explosion that rocketed them both at once.

Jenn's spine rose off the mattress and her head arched back with what seemed like a seismic force, even stopping her from breathing as she was gripped by something inexplicably stupendous and more earth-shattering than anything she'd ever known before, holding her suspended for what seemed like forever and not long enough at the same time.

And then it ebbed, threatened to come again, and ebbed once more.

Slowly, slowly, the chaos of her senses calmed and she lay back, exhausted and spent and aglow with something that seemed to Jenn to have transcended anything any mere mortal woman could ever expect as Matt, too, nearly collapsed above her.

They stayed there for a while longer, their bodies melded together, their limbs tangled and entwined, their hearts still racing in unison.

Then Matt rose up just enough to kiss her again. Sweetly but with a new closeness, a new sense of connection.

He smoothed her hair away from her brow where it had fallen in a riot of curls and kissed her forehead, too, as he slipped out of her.

Then he held her close and rolled to his back, keeping her tucked to his side so she could use his considerable shoulder as a pillow and he could lay his cheek to the top of her head.

It crossed her mind to make some kind of joke.

To say "Zorro strikes again" or "now that was a Christmas gift."

But she didn't. She didn't want anything to diffuse that moment, that bond they'd just forged.

And as they both relaxed and Matt's breathing deepened to such an extent that she knew he was falling asleep, she could only hope that nothing else could break the bond they'd forged, either.

That it could weather even the truth she would tell him in the morning.

Chapter Twelve

Matt woke up Christmas morning a happy man. The bedroom curtains were open and from Jenn's bed he could see bright blue sky and sunshine glimmering on the snow-covered wonderland outside. He could hear Evie Lee giggling and exclaiming over what she'd found under the tree in the suite of rooms adjacent to Jenn's.

And most of all, he had Jenn asleep in his arms. Everything felt right with the world.

Okay, maybe not quite everything. He still wished he knew more about Jenn's background, her history. But as he pulled the covers up over her bare shoulders and his naked chest and rested his cheek atop her head where it was snuggled against his neck, he was thinking that even though he didn't know much more about her than he had when he'd pulled her out of her snow-bound car, he could tell what sort of person she was.

That was what he'd meant the night before when he'd said maybe he knew all he needed to know about her.

He hadn't been referring to the few facts he had. Yes, it was important to know she wasn't married, that she didn't have kids she'd left behind. But wasn't it also important to know that she was kind and thoughtful and good-natured?

That she wasn't anything like Sarah had been?

Oh, yeah. That was the important part.

Because even though Sarah had done a good job with keeping secrets about herself, there had been other indications that she wasn't a woman he would have wanted in his life. Indications he had ignored that would have warned him earlier if he'd paid attention to them. Indications that she lacked character and integrity. That she was selfish and self-centered and self-indulgent. That she was her only real priority and that she had every intention of making sure she got whatever she wanted even if it was at someone else's expense.

But that wasn't Jenn.

Jenn was considerate to a fault. She'd pulled her own weight since coming to stay with the McDermots, whereas under the same circumstances, Sarah would have lounged around, milked her injuries and expected to be waited on hand and foot.

Jenn had put her own needs second to what other people wanted. There hadn't been a single time she hadn't been willing to go along with the majority rule, or to lend a hand, even when she wasn't completely up to it—like yesterday when she'd had that headache and it had taken the whole family ganging up on her to make her lie down.

And as for being selfish or self-centered? He'd spent more time thinking about her and her problems than she had.

Plus he'd seen the way she was with Evie Lee and Andrew. She was patient and calm and caring and perfectly happy letting them be center stage. Something Sarah would have competed mightily for.

And wasn't that what he was really looking for—a woman with all the qualities Jenn had? Matt asked himself.

He knew the answer without even having to think about it. Yes, Jenn did have all the qualities he was looking for in a woman.

So what difference did it make what was in her past?

He could hire a private detective to investigate it so they'd know exactly what she'd come from—and he would—but obviously since no one was looking for her or cared that she was missing, she must not have anyone special in her life. She must not have pressing obligations or binding commitments. She must not have strong ties.

And to Matt's way of thinking at that moment, that meant the field was open.

It meant that *he* could be the special someone in her life. The strong tie. The person who would care about her. Care for her.

As he lay there feeling her body fitted so perfectly to his that it seemed as if they'd been carved from the same stone, feeling the warmth of her breath against his skin, wanting her all over again, he thought, why not?

Why not be the special someone in her life? Why not be her strong tie? Why not be the person who cared about and for her?

He couldn't think of any reason why not.

Any more than not knowing about her past seemed to be any reason not to give in to his feelings for her anymore.

Because suddenly it seemed as though nothing that came before the day he'd found her mattered. That all that mattered was what was between them now.

And what was between them now was powerful.

Powerful enough to make him feel as if he could trust her. As if he could believe in her.

Believe in her enough to give his heart up to her.

Because he had faith that she'd treat the gift of his heart with care and compassion, and give her own heart in return.

So even though he might not know her inside and out, even though he might not know so much about her that she verged on the boring, he was willing to take a risk on her. On having a relationship with her.

On having a future with her.

Because feelings like he had for her didn't come along that often. And when they did, they were worth holding on to at almost any cost.

Jenn was worth holding on to at almost any cost.

At least he hoped she was. He hoped he wasn't wrong about her.

Because the truth was, at that moment, lying with her in his arms on that Christmas morning, he didn't think he could let her go even if he had to.

And he certainly couldn't imagine anything he could find out about her now that would make him want to.

"Santa comed! Santa comed! Santa comed!"

The sound of Evie Lee's joyous voice muted by the walls and coming from a distance was still enough to wake Jenn.

She knew instantly that it was Matt's warm body she was snuggled against. Matt's strong arms wrapped around her. Matt's head pressed to the top of hers.

And she couldn't help the little sigh of pleasure that escaped her because it felt like pure bliss to be there like that, with him.

"Sweet dreams?" he asked in a morning-raspy voice.

"Better than that," she said, rubbing her cheek against his shoulder.

He laughed a soft, sexy laugh and hugged her close.

"Have you been awake long?" she asked.

"Long enough."

Jenn craned her head back so she could peer up at him, at the rugged beauty of his whisker-shadowed face. "Long enough for what?" she inquired with a voice full of hopeful innuendo.

"For thinkin'," he answered with another laugh.

"Shall I offer a penny for your thoughts?"

"Nah, I'll give 'em to you for free. I was thinkin' about you and me and bein' together like this forever."

That put a damper on Jenn's spirits and it echoed in her, "Oh."

Not because the prospect of spending forever in his arms wasn't exactly what Jenn wanted. But it wasn't as simple as he made it sound.

He didn't seem to notice the change in her attitude or enthusiasm, though, as he continued. "I was thinkin' that since we know you're a free woman, the only thing that makes any difference is the here and now. And the future. The future we could have together. I was thinkin' that you could stay here at the ranch whether your memory comes back or not. That we could hire someone to find out whatever you want to know about yourself, tie up any loose ends you might have left in Denver and go on from here. You and I—"

"Wait," Jenn said, cutting him off before he could say more of what could have been music to her ears if things were as uncomplicated as he thought they were.

But she had to make good on her vow to herself the previous night to tell him first thing that her memory was back, to let him know all that involved. So she said, "I have to tell you something."

Matt looked down at her. "That doesn't sound good."

"Part of it isn't."

His brows nearly met over the bridge of his nose but the corners of his lips were still upturned in a tiny smile that made it look as if he didn't believe that anything she could say was all that serious. "Shoot."

Jenn took a deep breath and let it out slowly, praying for courage to do what she knew she had to do.

But now that the time was at hand she couldn't find the words. "This is so bad," she breathed more to herself than to him.

"Tell me," he urged.

She let her forehead rest in the palm of her own hand for a moment, fighting the guilt that flooded her. Guilt over not having told him sooner. Guilt over what she had to tell him.

"Jenn?" he prompted.

She took a deep breath, looked him in the eye and nearly whispered, "My memory came back."

That took his expression through a series of alterations, as if he wasn't sure whether the return of her memory was a good thing or not. Probably because she hadn't said it as if it were a good thing.

"When?" seemed to be all he could think to say.

"It started the day before yesterday, out of the blue," she began, still speaking quietly, as if that would soften the blow. She explained that the first memory to return had been Greta Banks's phone number, then went on to tell him about the call she'd made to her best friend and what Greta had told her. Then Jenn was frank about the fact that her memory had completely come back after the headache of the previous day.

Matt didn't say anything throughout her whole recounting. When she was finished, he sat up, bracing his back against the headboard and leaving her to fend for herself.

Jenn ended up clutching the sheet to her breasts with one hand and pushing herself up beside him, looking at the storm cloud of his handsome face and feeling strongly what seemed like his withdrawal from her.

But now that she'd begun this, she went on to fill him in on the details of herself as a single history professor who had lost the last of her family when her grandmother had died two weeks earlier.

What she didn't tell him was the worst of what she now knew, saving that for last.

But the time for telling that part came when he said, "And why were you on your way to Elk Creek?"

He already sounded injured and aloof and that didn't make it any easier to tell him the portion she really thought would alienate him.

But what choice did she have?

She didn't answer his question immediately, though. She slid to the edge of the bed, pulling the quilt around her like a toga as she crossed the room to the closet.

Inside the walk-in closet she did two things—she pulled on her bathrobe and took the old beat-up shaving kit out of her suitcase to bring with her back to bed.

But when she left the closet, she didn't find Matt still in bed.

He'd pulled on his black jeans and was waiting for her with one shoulder pressed to the window-pane, looking out at nothing she could see.

When he heard her step from the closet, he turned his head—only his head—to look at her.

And the frown on his handsome face wasn't encouraging.

Jenn swallowed her growing unease and handed him the shaving kit.

"What's this?"

"My grandmother's name was Gloria Munroe. She was born and raised in Elk Creek. And in love with your grandfather."

Matt opened the shaving kit and glanced inside. "Money?"

"Two thousand one hundred and fifty-seven dollars. It belonged to your grandfather. Something happened between them—my grandmother would never tell me what—but she took the money and used it to leave town, to start a new life for herself in Denver. I didn't know this until three days before she died. In fact, even though she always subscribed to Elk Creek's newspaper and told me she'd come from here originally, she wouldn't ever talk about that, either. She only told me about taking the money because she knew she was dying and it was very important to her that I return the money she'd taken. Not that that's the original cash. That's what she saved over the years until she had the exact amount she'd stolen, but she'd never been brave enough to bring it back herself. She said she'd felt too ashamed. But she wanted to make right what she'd done wrong and she made me promise I would return the money to Buzz after she died."

"And so here you are. Quite a coincidence that you ended up right where you were supposed to be."

There was sarcasm in his tone that shocked Jenn.

"You say that as if I manipulated it. But yes, it is a coincidence. How could it be anything else?"

He shrugged one of those broad, bare shoulders and Jenn fought not to notice just how gorgeous it was. Just how gorgeous was his entire bare chest and belly and back...

Matt didn't respond to her challenge about how their encountering each other could have been anything but a coincidence. He just stood there, staring at her, scowling at her, obviously not thrilled by what he'd heard.

Jenn felt the need to fill that silence with something, so she said, "I found the shaving kit in my suitcase that first day you brought me here and every time I saw it or thought about it, it gave me a bad feeling from then on. I didn't say anything to you because I was afraid I might have stolen the money or something."

"So you were keeping it a secret."

"I just didn't know what any of it might mean," she defended lamely, hearing the condemnation in his tone.

"And you thought it was better not to let me in on it."

"I thought it was better to wait a little while, until maybe I remembered something."

"So that if it was bad, you could keep it a secret indefinitely. Hope I never found out."

He went on staring at her, his forest-green eyes boring into her like lasers cutting to the quick. Only this time Jenn didn't say anything because it seemed as if opening her mouth only made things worse.

Then Matt said, "You know, I was thinkin' that there wasn't anything that could come up that was likely to make me want to let go of you. That you were different than Sarah. But now I find out you aren't different when it comes to keepin' secrets, are you?"

"It isn't the same thing," Jenn said, hating the slight note of pleading in her voice. But she *was* pleading. Pleading for him to understand, not to clump her into the same category with the woman who had hurt him with her deceptions.

But it didn't seem to matter as he continued with a full measure of disappointment in his tone. "It was one thing to accept that neither of us knew what was in your past. I was ready to act on just what we did know. But now you tell me I'm the only one of us who's been in the dark. That you knew. That you'd remembered, and just didn't bother to let me in on it. Like Sarah."

"I thought you might be put off by the fact that my grandmother stole from your grandfather. But that doesn't bother you as much as the fact that I didn't tell you I'd gotten my memory back the minute it happened, does it?'' she asked, just to clarify for herself.

''What your grandmother did to my grandfather was between them. You'll have to deal with whatever it is that that brings up for him. But you bet I'm put off by your keeping secrets. What else did you think I'd be? Happy about it?''

''It isn't the way you're making it sound. It isn't as if I never really had amnesia and have just been faking it to pull the wool over your eyes, or as if I didn't bother to tell you when I did remember. It wasn't an easy decision to postpone letting you know. I just didn't want to ruin everyone's Christmas Eve and party and—''

''And there wasn't a single thought about yourself in it,'' he said dubiously.

''Yes, there was a thought of me, too. I knew no one was going to be too happy about spending their holiday with the granddaughter of someone who had stolen from their grandfather. I figured Buzz would likely just kick me out on my ear—and who could blame him? But none of that was my first thought. My first thought was that it would ruin everyone's Christmas. Is that what you would have wanted me to do? To have brought it all out into the open minutes before your party began?''

His scowl only deepened. ''Maybe,'' he said. ''At least you could have told me even if you didn't let anyone else know.''

''And just ruin everything for you. Okay, maybe that's what I should have done. But I was afraid you wouldn't be too happy with the truth about who I am, and I wanted…'' It was hard to admit what had gone through her mind when she'd made that decision. But she knew that if there was any hope of salvaging this relationship she had to be completely honest with him. So she forged on. "I wanted just one more night before that happened."

"So you were thinking of yourself. Guess you got what you wanted then, didn't you? In spades."

His tone was so snide, so hurtful.

"Why is *when* I told you so important? It was only a few hours," she said, trying to make him put everything into perspective.

But that only seemed to bring more of his anger to the surface. "The fact that you intentionally kept the return of your memory a secret from me for even a few minutes means you deceived me. That's why it's so important. You made a choice and the choice you made was to keep secret something I should have been told."

"But it was only for a little while. To let things be nice for Christmas."

"That doesn't cut it with me. It doesn't matter how long you carried it out. It matters that you did it. A little while or a long while—it's all the same to me. Now I have to wonder what else you're not tellin' me. For whatever excuse you think you have."

"Or maybe what you're really angry about is that my memory coming back robbed you of the chance to hire an impartial third party to go out and document my life for you. Then you could have been reassured that it was true, that I wasn't covering anything up. Because anything short of that and you can't trust me or anybody else."

"I was ready to trust you even not knowing anything about your past."

"No, you weren't. You were ready to trust some private investigator. If you trusted me, you'd trust that I did what I thought was best for a short period of time and that what I did wasn't anything like someone not telling you she was married and had abandoned her kids in a gas station. You'd trust that my intentions were good and that they didn't have anything to do with deceiving you. You'd trust that I've told you everything there is to tell now. But that's not what you're saying."

"I'm saying you should have told me the truth. Right away. Because a lie of omission is still a lie. It's still deceit."

And that seemed to be that. His final words. His final proclamation. His final judgment of her.

And it was pretty harsh.

"I didn't feel like it was lying or deceiving. It wasn't as if I was feigning amnesia so you'd take me into your home, into your family, into your—" She'd almost said bed, but stopped herself. "It isn't as if I didn't tell you so I could take something from you or trap you into something or mislead you. I just postponed telling you so the holiday wasn't ruined for everyone."

"You didn't tell me because you figured it might turn me off—which is the same reason Sarah didn't tell me about herself."

There was some truth to that so how could she deny it?

She couldn't.

She could only say, "I'm sorry."

But it wasn't enough. She could see it in the tension in his face, in the disillusionment in his eyes.

Something tightened up and stabbed her so sharply inside she wanted to double over in response. To crawl away and hide. And cry.

Instead she stayed where she was, fighting the tears, trying to maintain some dignity.

"I'm sorry," she repeated in a quiet voice. "I'll get dressed, do what I came here to do and get out."

She wanted badly for him to say no. To tell her he didn't want her to do that. That he was mad but that he'd get over it. That he still cared about her. That he still wanted her in his life the way he had only moments before she'd told him the truth.

But he didn't do any of that. He didn't say anything.

And all she could think to say was another soft, "I'm sorry," as she watched him push away from the window and walk out of the room.

Chapter Thirteen

Matt was waiting outside Jenn's room when she opened her door an hour later. During that hour she'd showered and dressed, combed her hair and tried to camouflage the red splotches left from crying in the shower. Then she'd packed her bags and made arrangements for herself through two phone calls.

That had left nothing to do but find Buzz and tell him who she was and why she was there.

But the last thing she'd expected to find when she'd finally made herself head out of the safe confines of her rooms was Matt leaning against the wall in the hallway.

He'd showered and dressed, too. He had on a pair

of dark blue jeans and a dove-gray Western shirt, and his face was freshly shaved.

But he didn't look any happier with her now than he had when he'd left her before. Especially not the way he was leaning, as if he were holding up the wall with his shoulders, his arms crossed over his broad chest.

"I told the old man you need to speak to him in private. He's waitin' in the den," Matt informed her without preamble.

Jenn hadn't realized that opening her door to him had raised her hopes but clearly it had because she felt them deflate all over again with that monotone greeting.

She held her head high so he couldn't see the effect and said, "Good."

Matt pushed off the wall then and nodded his dimpled chin in the direction of the den, motioning for her to go ahead of him.

She didn't know why he was involving himself in this but there was an air of protectiveness about him that made her assume he was running interference for his grandfather to ensure Buzz wasn't upset by her.

So, with shaving kit in hand, Jenn walked down the hall, feeling as if she were going to the gallows.

"There you are," Buzz said the minute he spotted her in the doorway when she reached the den. "I hear you want to see me."

The elderly man's tone was friendly enough, telling Jenn that Matt hadn't filled his grandfather in on any of the details.

That was left to her and she wasted no time getting down to business as Matt closed the door behind them and went to stand like a sentry beside the easy chair Buzz occupied.

As she said her piece the old man's expression sobered and Jenn shored up for a second helping of McDermot wrath.

But that wasn't what Buzz dished out when she finished.

Instead he shook his head sadly and said, "The shame was mine."

"Yours?" Jenn said, surprised.

"Mine. All mine," the elderly man confirmed. "Somethin' terrible happened to your grandma and I didn't take it as serious as I should've. She left because she was afraid and she had good reason to be."

"Afraid of you?"

That made him chuckle wryly. "No, not of me. Back then the mayor's son was our age. J.D. we called 'im. Nobody liked 'im much but Gloria was scared of 'im. I didn't understand why. He seemed harmless enough to me, so I pooh-poohed everything she told me 'bout him followin' her around and watchin' her. Figured everybody knew me and her was engaged to be married and so what if J.D. was doin' a little lookin'. Gloria was a pretty girl. Like you."

Jenn didn't respond to the compliment but Buzz didn't notice as he went on.

"One night Gloria was walkin' home from choir practice at the church and out pops J.D. He got a might too friendly before somebody happened by and shooed him off. 'Course when Gloria told me, I went after him, gave him what-for, and I figured that took care of it. But Gloria just couldn't rest about it. She tried even more to tell me how scared she was of J.D. but I didn't pay it any mind. When she started talkin' 'bout our leavin' town to get away from 'im, I thought she was crazy. Said no way I was leavin' Elk Creek just because some backward boy tried stealin' a kiss. That was when she took the money and left.''

Buzz shook his head again, looking off into space as if he were lost in old memories and had forgotten Jenn and Matt were even there.

''That money was my gettin' hitched money,'' he said after a moment. ''Didn't trust banks. Kept it in my old shavin' kit under the bed. 'Course Gloria knew 'bout it, knew where it was. One day not long after J.D.'d bothered 'er she just up and disappeared. And so did the money.''

Buzz shook his head again. ''I was plenty mad. And hurt. But I came to know that she was right to do it. 'Bout a year later J.D. had his sights set on another girl. Only nobody happened by to shoo him off that time and he forced himself on 'er. When her father found her—beaten up and… well, in no shape a father should ever have to find his daughter, she told 'im it was J.D.'d done it. Her father went after J.D. and shot 'im dead.

''To my way of thinkin' it was no more'n J.D. deserved, but the man spent the rest of his life in jail for it. Then, to make matters worse, J.D.'d got the girl in a family way from that attack. She couldn't stand the thought of havin' a baby she'd come by like that, tried to do away with it before it was born and died in the process. And all I could think was that that girl could've been Gloria. That Gloria was right to get out of here, away from J.D. before that happened to her. And I was just a damn fool for not havin' paid attention to what she was tellin' me. So losin' the money was no more'n I deserved.''

Buzz seemed to return from his thoughts then and he looked more closely at Jenn. "Yep. That's why you looked familiar to me. She's there around the nose and mouth. My Gloria.''

Jenn gave him the best smile she could manage under the circumstances, relieved in spite of everything to know Buzz didn't hate her grandmother the way her grandmother had been sure he must.

Then she handed Buzz the shaving kit. "My grandmother's favorite saying was that everything happens for a reason. I'm sure she'd have said that now, too, and believed that the two of you must just not have been meant to be together. Probably so you could make the family you did and she could make the one she did.''

"And maybe so those two families could come together now," the elderly man suggested hopefully, looking from Jenn to Matt and back again.

But when Matt didn't move a muscle to acknowledge that possibility, Jenn ignored the comment, too, and instead said, "Well, that's what I came here to do. I guess now I'd better get back to my room. The sheriff's deputy is on his way out here to pick me up. Once the snow melts enough to get my car out of the ditch, I'll be going back to Denver. But I appreciate all your hospitality and your being so understanding about the money. I think my grandmother will rest easier now.''

Once more Buzz looked to his grandson expectantly.

And once more nothing happened.

But Jenn wasn't going to stand there hoping for a reprieve that wasn't coming, so she drew herself up and spoke to Buzz as if Matt weren't there at all, ''Please tell everyone goodbye and thank you for everything.''

''I'll do that,'' the old man assured even though he was still looking at Matt. Then he nodded his head in Jenn's direction, urging his grandson to do something.

But still Matt didn't budge or make a sound.

So Jenn said a last goodbye to Buzz, turned and left the room and both men behind.

''You just gonna let 'er go like that, boy?''

Buzz had waited until Jenn was out of the den and the door was closed behind her before he'd spoken directly to Matt.

But Matt was a little slow on the uptake. It wasn't easy to focus on his grandfather's words when he felt as if a vise were twisting his insides in a vicious grip.

''Yes, sir, I am,'' he finally answered. With conviction.

"Then yer as big a damn fool as I was nearly sixty years ago. What the hell's goin' on with you this mornin'? Up to now you been googly-eyed over that girl and now you won't even look at 'er. And why's she leavin'? Don't none of this make sense."

Matt debated about confiding in the old man. About wearing his heart on his sleeve, which was not his way.

But even though it wasn't his way, he needed to get this off his chest and so in the end he gave in and let Buzz know exactly what spur was under his saddle and why. And what he'd done about it.

"Fool," Buzz snarled.

"I've been burned once by a woman who kept secrets and deceived me. I won't let it happen again."

Somewhere in talking about what had happened between himself and Jenn since waking up, Matt had moved to sit on the leather sofa at a right angle to his grandfather. He had one ankle propped on the opposite knee and he was staring at his cowboy-booted foot rather than at his grandfather. But he still saw Buzz's head shaking.

Then Buzz said, "You know, I didn't do right by that girl's grandmom all those years past. I didn't listen to what she was tellin' me. I dug in my heels into my own way of lookin' at things, and my stubbornness cost me a woman I loved. Now don't get me wrong—I met your grandmother later on and I loved her, too. Like there was no tomorrow. But I did wrong by Gloria and I lost 'er. And there was always a part of me that regretted that, that never stopped thinkin' 'bout 'er. Your Jenn's a good girl and yer losin' her just as surely—take it from somebody who knows from experience. And you'll be just as sorry."

Buzz poked the bottom of Matt's boot with the end of his cane. "Hear what I'm tellin' you, boy?"

Then he got to his feet and walked out of the den, leaving Matt alone with his thoughts.

And the gut-wrenching pain he was fighting.

He was glad things had worked out for Buzz over that money. Glad Jenn's returning it hadn't raised ugly memories, or hard feelings, or old resentments. For his grandfather's sake.

But that didn't have any effect on what was going on with Matt. It didn't alter the fact that Jenn hadn't told him right away that she'd regained her memory, that she'd kept everything a secret until it suited her to tell him.

So maybe he did have his heels dug in pretty deep, but he had good reason for it.

Well, he had reason for it, although apparently he was alone in thinking it was *good* reason.

But dammit all to hell, no one else had gone through what he'd gone through with Sarah. The disillusionment. The disappointment. The pain of finding out she wasn't what he'd thought she was.

He'd felt every bit of that all over again that morning when he'd found out Jenn had been keeping secrets of her own.

So okay, she hadn't kept them long. And unlike Sarah, Jenn had told him herself what was going on, he hadn't had to find it out from someone else. But still...

That last thought jammed in his brain and stalled the headlong rush of his mind as he realized what he'd just hit upon.

Old Buzz would have said, "But still nothin'," he thought, realizing only then that the fact that Jenn had told him the truth—even if somewhat belatedly—was a big deal. A very big deal. That it was much different than what Sarah had done and he hadn't seen it until that moment.

Because not only hadn't Sarah offered him the information about herself, she'd even tried to deny everything when Matt had confronted her. And it had been more than clear that she would never have told him the truth if she hadn't been forced to.

But Jenn had. Voluntarily. Willingly.

Just not promptly.

Because she was different than Sarah.

That was the conclusion he'd come to when he'd awakened with Jenn in his arms that morning and now it struck him all over again. Only with more force.

Jenn was different than Sarah.

A lot different, he admitted to himself anew.

Before he'd found out that she hadn't told him her memory had returned he'd thought that he knew what sort of person she was—kind, considerate, compassionate, good-natured, good-hearted, unselfish.

Now he had to ask himself if any of that had

changed just because for a few hours she hadn't told him the amnesia had lifted.

And the answer was no, it hadn't changed. In fact, it suddenly seemed ridiculous to even think such a thing. She was still the same person. She'd just had what, at its worst, could be considered a brief lapse in judgment.

And it probably wouldn't have even been considered that if he wasn't so sensitive to certain things.

But he was, and that sensitivity had definitely caused him to dig in his heels, to not even listen to her reasoning, her explanation. To not acknowledge her point of view.

But he hadn't listened to her point of view because he'd been thinking that anything and everything she said was a lie by then. That he would always have to wonder what she wasn't telling him, or if what she was telling him was the truth.

But was *that* true? Would he always have to wonder if she was being open and honest with him?

That gave him pause. He'd meant it when he'd said it to her, but now that he'd cooled off some, it seemed pretty extreme.

She hadn't actually outright lied to him the way Sarah had.

Jenn had only postponed telling him about herself. By less than a day. And when he thought about it now, that didn't seem to be a sign of a deceitful or secretive nature. It didn't mean that what she'd told him wasn't true. Maybe he'd been a little heavy-handed with all that lie-by-omission stuff and the accusations of deceit.

Matt finally had to admit that to himself.

He didn't believe that he had any cause to doubt her forever just because of this one thing. This one thing she'd done with other people in mind. Because unlike Sarah, Jenn *did* think of other people…

Matt ran his hands over his face as if he were washing it, pulling down hard on his skin, punishing himself for losing sight of so much. For somehow even losing sight of his feelings for Jenn.

Yes, he'd loved Sarah. That was why it had hit him so hard when he'd learned what was really going on with her.

But his feelings for Jenn were even stronger. Deeper. More abiding. They really were the kind of feelings that didn't come along often. The kind that were worth holding on to when they did.

It had been true before and it was true now.

And so was the fact that Jenn was worth holding on to. Just the way her grandmother had been. At any cost.

And if that cost was loosening up a little? If that cost was swallowing some pride and letting go of her sin of temporary omission?

It wasn't a high price to pay.

It sure as hell wasn't as high a price as losing her the way Buzz had lost her grandmother.

"Damn!" Matt muttered to himself, wondering how he'd let so much of the past get in the way of the present and knowing that if he didn't act quickly it was going to do even more damage.

So he shot up out of his seat and made a beeline

for the den door, hoping to high heaven he wasn't already too late.

But when he got to Jenn's rooms they were filled only with the bright sunshine reflected off the snow.

Because Jenn was already gone.

Jenn had requested the services of the sheriff's deputy to take her to Elk Creek's boardinghouse because she hadn't known anyone else to ask for a ride. He'd been obliging and so had Lurlene and Effie Partridge, who owned the boardinghouse and had shown her to a flowery blue room on the second floor of their old Victorian house.

The Partridge sisters had invited her to join the rest of the household for eggnog, but Jenn had politely declined and instead secluded herself in her room. She just didn't have the heart nor the energy for socializing.

Once she'd set down her suitcase and removed her coat, she made her way to the dormer window and leaned against the framework there to look down on the Partridge's backyard and Elk Creek beyond it.

She realized that she'd fallen in love with the small town even before she'd come here, but now it seemed to hold only pain for her.

So lost in that pain and misery was she that the knock on her door that came some time later didn't register at first. And when it did, she didn't move away from the window to answer it. She didn't even ask who it was. She just willed whoever it was to go away, hoping that without a response they would think she was napping.

But there was a second, louder knock that was too insistent to ignore, and after taking a deep, resigned breath, she said a weak, "Yes?"

The door opened without announcement and there was Matt, standing in the hallway.

Jenn's first inclination was to look beyond him, wondering if he'd brought the sheriff back to arrest her for something. Was it illegal to return sixty-year-old ill-gotten gains?

But there was no sign of the sheriff. There was only Matt. Looking heart-stoppingly handsome but as if he'd run all the way into town from the ranch.

"A talent for disappearing acts must run in your family," he said then.

"I didn't disappear. I just left," she said lamely.

"Good thing this is a small town and there's only one place you could go."

"Why? Did I forget something you had to track me down for?"

"No, you didn't forget anything. I did," he answered in a deep voice.

The only thing she could think of that he might have forgotten was to take back the beautiful bracelet he'd given her for Christmas. But she was one step ahead of him.

"I left it on the coffee table where it was last night," she informed him, trying hard not think about how much she'd liked the bracelet, or the way they'd spent the time after she'd received it.

"You left what on the coffee table?" he asked, frowning at her.

"The bracelet. I knew you wouldn't want me to have it."

Light dawned in Matt's expression but he shook his head. "That's not what I forgot."

"What then?" she asked, confused herself now.

"Can I come in?" he asked rather than answering her question.

Jenn just shrugged when what she really felt like doing was squirming beneath the intensity of his penetrating gaze.

Matt took the shrug as her concession and stepped into the room, closing the door behind him.

And that was when he said, "What I forgot is you."

"Me?"

"Mmm. I forgot that you are who you are. That you aren't someone else."

Seeing him in the hall outside her room when she'd opened the door to go to Buzz had raised and lowered her hopes too painfully to want to go through that emotional roller coaster again, so she kept a tight hold on any hopes that threatened in response to what he seemed to be saying. She merely waited for him to explain.

"I'm not usually an idiot," he finally continued. "But this morning... This morning I think maybe I have been. I woke up before you did and started thinkin' about you, about us, about not knowing much about you, and by the time you were stirring I'd come to the conclusion that it didn't matter what

I didn't know about you because I knew *you*—the kind of person you are—and that between that and my feelings for you, it was enough.''

''And then I let you know I hadn't told you about the amnesia going away,'' Jenn filled in, thinking that she was hearing an apology but not anything more. Refusing to allow herself to entertain even a fantasy that it might be more.

''And that pushed a bad button in me,'' he confirmed. ''Just that quick you didn't seem like who I'd decided you were. You were Sarah all over again.''

''But I'm not,'' she defended herself reflexively, before she'd even thought about it.

''I know you aren't. Now. Old Buzz just gave me a tongue-lashing and started me thinkin' all over again. And that was when I got my memory back and realized again you are who you are.''

He paused and Jenn thought he was just going to wrap up his apology and say goodbye.

But instead he said, ''And I'm in love with who you really are.''

That shocked her so much it took her breath away. In her wildest dreams that wasn't what she'd expected to hear from him.

''You are?'' she said, hating that she sounded so stunned.

He laughed at her tone and probably at the wide-eyed surprise that went with it. ''Yeah, I am. In fact, it didn't occur to me just how much in love with you I am until a few minutes ago when I started thinkin' about losing you the way my grandfather had lost your grandmother. And I couldn't stand the idea of your goin' off the way she did, to a whole lifetime with somebody else.''

"There isn't anybody else," she said, again more a reflex than anything, to assure him she honestly wasn't Sarah and she honestly didn't have anything to hide from him.

"I'm sorry, Jenn. I was an idiot to blow this whole thing out of proportion. I'm not sayin' I don't hate that you didn't tell me about your memory comin' back right away—I have a sore spot when it comes to anybody keepin' me in the dark for any amount of time. But I can see now that you had your reasons and since you did finally tell me on your own... Well, it sure as hell isn't enough to throw away what we have between us. Not for me, anyway. Maybe I'm too big an idiot for you?''

Jenn stared at him, taking in the sight of that incredibly handsome face of sharp planes and chiseled features, feasting on the vision of his unruly hair, drinking in the glory of that sculpted, powerfully muscled body she craved even at that moment, and she thought about how much his rejection had hurt her.

He had hurt her. But was it enough to destroy what they'd begun together?

She didn't need to consider that for long.

Because just looking at him was enough to make her heart flip-flop with what she felt for him and she realized that she'd fallen in love with Matt, too. Deeply in love with him.

"I think I can forgive you for being an idiot if

you can forgive me for keeping my secret," she finally said.

"Done."

He crossed the room to her then, reaching for her hand when he got to her to pull her into his arms.

"Now I'm gonna tell you what I *really* want for Christmas," he said.

Jenn glanced in the direction of the bed.

Matt saw it and laughed. "What *else* I want for Christmas."

"Okay."

"Kiss me first," he ordered.

She did, using the balm of his lips to soothe nerves that were still on edge and hadn't yet fully accepted what was happening now.

Then Matt said, "I love you."

The words made Jenn smile and tears rush to her eyes.

She blinked them away and said, "I love you, too."

He sighed elaborately. "Thank goodness. You had me worried." He peered down into her eyes with a softness in those dark green depths that warmed her right to the core. "Will you marry me?"

Yet another surprise of the morning.

"Are you serious?"

"I'm not kiddin', that's for sure."

"Marry you?"

"Yep. Stay here and make an honest man of me now that you've had your way with me."

"Well, if you put it like that I guess I'll have to," she joked, trying to regain her bearings.

He squeezed her. "Say it nicer than that."

This time she laughed. "I would love to marry you," she said more seriously. "But are you sure?"

She couldn't help adding that last part, remembering how angry he'd been with her such a short time before.

Apparently he understood from where her insecurity originated because he made a somber, sincerely contrite face and rested his brow on the top of her head. "Oh, I'm so sorry I made you feel bad," he said in a hushed voice. "Yes, I'm sure. I've never been more sure of anything. I love you, Jenn. I want you for my wife. I want to spend all of eternity with you. And I'll do my damnedest never, ever to hurt you again."

The tears sprang up once more and this time they were harder for Jenn to blink away.

But when she'd managed she said in a quiet voice of her own, "I love you and I would very much like to be your wife and spend all of eternity with you, too. And I'll do my damnedest never to hurt you again, either."

He kissed her a second time, this one tender and sweet and deep enough to sweep them up into a passion so intense Jenn wondered how either of them ever thought it might be denied. A passion that melded them together, that had hands caressing and exploring and claiming, and hearts pounding, and desires coming fast to life.

Matt tore his mouth from hers then and took his turn glancing toward the bed. "As appealing as that other gift you were offerin' to give me a minute ago is, I made everybody at home promise to wait to open gifts until I could find you and try gettin' you home to be part of the festivities.''

''You made those little kids wait?''

''The family wouldn't be complete without you,'' he said, kissing her again, long, slow, deep.

''I do love you, Jenn,'' he said when the kiss ended.

''I love you, too,'' she repeated.

''But we'd better get back before Evie Lee has our hides,'' Matt said.

''We'd better,'' Jenn agreed, only too happy to comply. After all, she was headed for something she'd never had before—a holiday with a big, loving family she was going to be a part of.

As Matt grabbed her suitcase and she put on her coat again, she knew that she genuinely had come home the day she'd met him.

And that, in a way, her grandmother had given her one final, miraculous gift.

The gift of Matt and the life they'd have together from that one wonderful Christmas Day on.

* * * * *

*Look for the next installment
in Victoria Pade's popular*
RANCHING FAMILY *series,*
COWBOY'S BABY,
*available in Silhouette Special Edition
in April 2001.*